Like

by

Jay Northcote

# Copyright

Cover artist: Garrett Leigh.
Editor: Sue Adams.
Like a Lover © 2015 Jay Northcote.

ALL RIGHTS RESERVED

This literary work may not be reproduced or transmitted in any form or by any means, including electronic or photographic reproduction, in whole or in part, without express written permission. This is a work of fiction and any resemblance to persons, living or dead, or business establishments, events or locales is coincidental.
The Licensed Art Material is being used for illustrative purposes only.
All Rights Are Reserved. No part of this may be used or reproduced in any manner whatsoever without written permission, except in the case of brief quotations embodied in critical articles and reviews.

Warning
This book contains material that is intended for a mature, adult audience. It contains graphic language, explicit sexual content, and adult situations.

# CHAPTER ONE

Josh sipped at his drink and tapped his foot impatiently on the rung of the bar stool as he watched the door.

Philip was nearly half an hour late now.

He checked his phone, to see if a message could have magically — and silently — appeared since he'd last looked at it five minutes ago, but the screen remained obstinately blank.

Philip was never late. He was one of Josh's regular clients, a businessman who was often in Plymouth for meetings. Josh had seen him every few weeks for over a year now, and he was always on time for their appointments. At least Josh had arranged to meet him tonight in a bar near the hotel rather than waiting in the room for him, so he could have a drink while he waited. Philip had paid in advance, so Josh wouldn't be out of pocket for the room, but Josh had been hoping for a quick appointment. He'd been up till the small hours finishing an essay last night, and he was knackered this evening. Yawning all over a client was never very professional. Thank God it was Saturday tomorrow, and he could sleep in.

He felt uneasy, though. This was uncharacteristic of Philip, so Josh couldn't help worrying. Josh didn't get emotionally attached to his clients. He couldn't do this job if he did. But Philip was one of the good guys. Charming, always courteous, he treated Josh like a person, not just a hole to fuck. Josh hoped he was okay and that nothing bad had happened.

He put his phone down on the bar and sighed. Glancing along the polished wood, he spotted another man a few metres down, sitting alone with a phone in his hand and a frown on his handsome face. Josh wondered whether he'd been stood up too.

Fifteen minutes later, Josh's glass was empty. By now he was sure Philip wouldn't show, but he didn't want to go home yet.

He didn't usually cruise for clients anymore. They came to him via his website. He preferred it that way, getting the booking up front. But tonight he felt restless. He'd been looking forward to a good fuck despite his tiredness. It would make him sleep better after, and Philip was always a guarantee of satisfaction. Maybe he could find someone else to provide that, and make a bit of extra cash while he was at it.

Josh could always use more money in his bank account. Being a student was an expensive business these days. With no financial support from his waste-of-space father, Josh had come to university facing the gloomy prospect of huge loans that would take him most of his working life to pay off. He'd been determined to get a job and work as many hours as he could fit around his studies, to relieve some of the financial burden. But he'd soon realised that working as a waiter or in a supermarket wasn't going to make much of a dent on his expenses.

Eventually he'd got a job working as a dancer in a gay club, and when men started to offer him money for sex, he'd figured why not?

Josh sat facing the bar now, his back to the door. He'd given up watching for Philip. Instead he let his gaze roam along the mirror behind the rows of bottles and glasses until he caught sight of the reflection of the man seated along the bar from him, still alone.

Josh studied him, admiring the high cheekbones and square jaw sprinkled with sand-coloured stubble and the thick mop of dark red hair that shone bright auburn where the light caught it. As Josh looked, the guy raised his eyes and caught Josh watching him in the mirror. He held Josh's gaze for a moment, and then he smiled, a hesitant but devastating curve of his lips that caused a twist of warmth to curl in the pit of Josh's belly.

*Well, hello.*

Josh smiled back. He didn't need to fake interest in this man. He was gorgeous and was clearly eyeing up Josh. He was well dressed, and with the prices of the drinks in this bar, he must be reasonably well off. It had to be worth a try.

Slipping off his barstool, Josh picked up his phone and approached the man, who turned to greet him.

"Hi," Josh said. "Mind if I join you?"

"Help yourself." The man gestured to the stool beside him. "But you looked as if you were waiting for someone."

"I was," Josh replied. "But I've given up on him now."

The man's lips quirked ruefully. "So we've both been stood up, then?"

"Looks that way. I'm Josh." He offered his hand.

"Rupert."

His hand was big and his grip firm. Josh deliberately let the tips of his fingers slide over Rupert's warm, smooth palm when he took his hand back. If Josh had been in any doubt that Rupert liked dick, the sweep of those cool blue eyes and the way they lingered for a moment too long on the crotch of Josh's skinny charcoal jeans would have been the deciding factor.

"Maybe their loss is our gain," Josh said with a grin.

"Maybe." Rupert looked amused, and then he added, "Can I buy you another drink, Josh?"

"Lime and soda please."

Once Rupert had ordered Josh's drink and another whisky for himself, he led the way to a table in the corner, away from the bar.

"So, who were you supposed to be meeting tonight? A date?" Rupert asked.

"Something like that." Josh didn't want to show his hand too soon. He knew from experience it was best to establish a connection first. "You?"

"Yeah, someone I'd met online. Maybe he chickened out of coming. Or maybe he saw me through the window and decided he didn't like the look of me." He chuckled ruefully.

"I doubt that." Josh held Rupert's gaze and let the tip of his tongue slip out to toy with the silver ring that pierced his bottom lip. Rupert tracked the movement and his pupils dilated. "More likely he saw you and felt inadequate."

Rupert flushed, surprising Josh. His slight bashfulness only made him more appealing, though.

Rupert changed the subject. "So, Josh. What do you do?"

"I'm a student. Politics and Economics. You?"

"I work in IT."

Josh was surprised. Rupert didn't look like his idea of a computer nerd. In his expensive-looking lightweight suit and crisp pale blue shirt, Rupert looked as though he'd come straight from an office or a bank.

"At the university," Rupert added.

"I wouldn't have guessed. I always thought IT guys were more jeans and T-shirts than sharp suits." He let his gaze skim over Rupert.

"Ah, but this" — Rupert gestured to his attire — "is because my mother was in town and I had to meet her for dinner earlier." His tone suggested it had been a duty meeting rather than a pleasurable one.

But Josh didn't react. He wanted to keep the conversation light. "Well, it suits you." He gave Rupert a flirty grin.

"Thanks." Rupert's cheeks went pink again. He had fair skin, so it was obvious every time he blushed.

They chatted for a while about the university. The conversation was a little stilted at first, but Josh was used to dealing with men who were shy or uncomfortable, so he persevered, gradually drawing Rupert out until he relaxed and started to talk more freely. Rupert had been living and working in Plymouth since September. He'd done a degree in London and then moved to work in Exeter for a couple of years. "I'm gradually working my way farther west... away from the clutches of my mother."

There was that tone again.

"Is she that bad?" Josh had no memory of his own mother. He'd grown up envying anyone who had a mum, no matter how much they complained about them.

Rupert grimaced. "Only in that she disapproves of everything I am and every single choice I've made. I don't think I could be more of a disappointment to her if I tried."

"Oh." Josh had no idea what to say because he didn't know how that might feel. His own father took no interest in anything Josh did. Josh didn't think it was be possible to disappoint his dad when he had zero expectations.

Rupert seemed to realise he was killing the mood and rallied quickly. "Sorry, sorry. You don't want to hear about my mother issues. Jesus." He moved his chair closer to Josh's and their knees touched under the small table. Josh wondered whether it was intentional. "I was supposed to be commiserating with you over our failed dates."

Josh lost himself in the blue of Rupert's eyes again. Tendrils of heat spread through him. "You were."

"I like your lip ring," Rupert said. His gaze dropped lower to Josh's collarbones. "What are your tattoos of?"

"Swallows." Rupert would just be able to see the wing tips that showed in this low-necked T-shirt. "Two of them."

"Have you got any other tattoos?"

Josh gave a slow, teasing smile. "Maybe. Do you want me to show you?"

Rupert met his eyes again. There was a flicker of uncertainty before he answered. "Yes. I'd like that."

Josh turned over the possibilities in his mind. It had been a long time since he'd had sex for anything other than for money. He usually saw clients at least three nights a week. They scratched the itch for him, and he didn't have the time or inclination to hook up with other guys. He hadn't dated since he'd started working as an escort. Josh didn't like lying about his job, but most guys didn't want to date escorts.

It would be easy to pick Rupert up tonight, though, and have no-strings sex with him for fun rather than cash. But Josh's rent was due.

"Me too. But it'll cost you," he finally said.

Rupert frowned, obvious confusion crossing his features as he tried to make sense of Josh's words. "What? I don't—"

"You're hot, and I wish I could do this without asking you for money. But a client let me down this evening. I have a hotel room booked and paid for next door, and I need someone to cover the cost for me." The lie came smoothly. "I can't afford to have sex for free tonight."

Rupert's mouth dropped open. Shock was evident on his face, but there was something else that was harder to read. His cheeks flooded pink again and his eyes went dark. "You're...." His voice came out husky, and he cleared his throat. "You're a...."

"A sex worker. An escort, to be precise. Hooker, rent boy, you get the gist. I'm an expensive one too. But my clients think I'm worth the money." Josh waited, tension making a muscle tick in his jaw as he forced himself to stay still and hold Rupert's gaze. On the occasions he'd tried picking up clients face-to-face, their reactions had varied.

Interest, anger, excitement, disgust... he'd seen them all. He steeled himself, ready for rejection.

Rupert licked his lips. "How much?" he finally asked.

"Two hundred for the first hour, one hundred for each extra hour after that."

Josh had started out charging much less at first, but quickly realised there was a market for his emo-twink look. Once he'd set up his website with some classy photos that showed him off to his best advantage, he'd hiked up his prices. He'd found charging higher rates only made him more appealing to a certain type of client.

There was a long pause, and Josh was sure Rupert was going to say no. He was positive Rupert had never paid anyone for sex before; his shocked reaction made that obvious.

"Okay." Josh made a move to stand. "I won't waste any more of your time, then."

Rupert shot out his hand and grabbed Josh's wrist, stopping him. "I'll pay," he said quietly. "But I don't have enough cash on me."

Excitement flooded Josh, not just at the thought of the money, but also at the thought of getting Rupert alone in a hotel room for an hour. He relaxed back into his seat again and picked up his drink. "There's a cashpoint over the road. I'll wait here while you get some."

"Right. I'll, uh, go and do that, then." Rupert stood abruptly, then picked up his double whisky and drained it in one gulp, obviously in need of liquid courage. Josh hid his smirk. "I'll be back in a minute."

Josh watched Rupert's very nice-looking arse as he walked away. He had a feeling this unexpected appointment wouldn't be too much of a hardship.

## CHAPTER TWO

Rupert's hands shook and his heart raced as he entered his PIN number at the cash machine. What the fuck was he doing? Was he really going to go through with this? He cursed as he got an error message, and tried again, more carefully this time.

He pressed the button for cash without a receipt and debated for a moment. Was one hour with Josh going to be enough?

*Fuck it.*

If he was doing this, he was going to do it properly. He withdrew four hundred pounds, just in case. He wanted to keep his options open.

When he walked back into the bar, Josh was looking at his phone again. Slouching back in his chair with his long slender legs stretched out under the table, he looked utterly relaxed. The polar opposite of how Rupert was feeling right now. Josh's dark fringe hung over his forehead. When he raised his head to greet Rupert, Josh's face lit up, his sharp features softening into a smile that made Rupert's stomach flip with nerves and desire.

"He finally texted," Josh said, putting his phone down on the table. "My client, I mean. I was a bit worried about him. He's usually ultrareliable, but he was stuck in a late meeting, and then his phone ran out of battery."

"I've got the money," Rupert said. He didn't want to hear about the man Josh was supposed to be meeting. Josh was *his* now, at least for the next few hours. That thought was satisfying in a way

Rupert could never have anticipated. Owning another person, buying the right to touch them. Who knew that would turn him on so much? But he'd been half-hard ever since Josh had named his price. "Are you ready to leave?"

If Rupert taking control of the situation surprised Josh, he didn't show it.

"Okay," he said mildly. He picked up his drink and downed what was left of it. His throat bobbed as he swallowed, and he licked his lips and gave Rupert a dirty grin. "Let's go."

Rupert imagined those lips around his cock and had to look away. These trousers didn't hide much, and with his shirt tucked in and his jacket hanging open, there was nothing to help hide his arousal. The sooner he got Josh somewhere alone, the better.

Josh followed him out into the street. It was nearly ten at night and mild for April. Orange street lamps lit the pavement, and the scent of the city streets filled Rupert's nostrils as he breathed in.

"This way." Josh turned towards one of the large chain hotels, popular with business visitors and tourists.

"Do you always see your... customers in a hotel room?" Rupert asked. The idea of Josh with these nameless, faceless men — Rupert assumed they were all men — made him feel a strange mix of excited and uneasy.

"I'm less likely to get arrested that way. Clients rarely want to bring an escort back to their home, and I wouldn't go even if they did. In the hotel there are security cameras in the corridors." He glanced sideways at Rupert as though assessing the risk.

Rupert supposed he was an unknown quantity. He was glad Josh was careful. "I guess that's sensible."

"I learned my lesson fast." Josh's tone was light—too light. Rupert wondered what had happened to make him so cautious now.

They made their way through the large double doors of the hotel and crossed the lobby to the lifts. The female receptionist looked up as they passed her, and smiled in recognition when Josh nodded.

Rupert felt his cheeks heat as her gaze slid over him, and his skin crawled with the realisation that she *knew*. She knew he'd be paying Josh to... to what? To suck him, to let Rupert fuck him? Or maybe he'd fuck Rupert if Rupert asked him to. He wondered what Josh's limits were: what *wouldn't* he do? Hot with shame, Rupert only felt more turned on.

The lift pinged, and the doors opened. Rupert followed Josh in and waited as he pressed the button for the fifth floor. When the doors slid shut, they were finally alone.

Unable to wait any longer, Rupert stepped in close to Josh and pinned up him against the mirrored wall. Nose to nose they were almost the same height. Rupert had maybe one inch on Josh, but Rupert was much broader and more powerful. Josh's eyes were green, strikingly beautiful, and his breath was soft on Rupert's lips as he waited for Rupert to make a move.

"You can kiss me," Josh finally said. "This isn't *Pretty Woman*, you know."

His mocking tone spurred Rupert into action, and he shut Josh up with a kiss, forcing Josh's lips apart so he could taste him as he slid both hands into Josh's hair. Josh's mouth was hot and sleek, opening greedily for Rupert's tongue. Josh grabbed Rupert's hips and tugged him in closer, giving a little moan that ramped Rupert's arousal up even higher. Rupert wondered if Josh was really into this, or if he was putting on an act. This was his job, after all. Rupert pulled away, breathing hard.

"Why'd you stop?" Josh murmured, eyes gratifyingly glazed. "That was hot."

If he was faking arousal, he was bloody good at it, but Rupert wanted to be sure. "I bet you say that to all the boys." He brought a hand down to cup the bulge in Josh's jeans. Josh was definitely hard. Not all an act, then. Rupert found the tip with his thumb and rubbed it, making Josh gasp and arch towards him just as the lift lurched to a stop.

"This is our floor." Josh pushed Rupert's hand away. "Hands to yourself till we're in the room. I don't want to get banned from the hotel for public indecency."

Rupert chuckled. "Okay. I think I can manage that."

He followed Josh down the corridor and waited while Josh made a couple of failed attempts with the key card.

Rupert snatched it out of his hand. "Let me try…. There." The light on the door finally flashed green, and he turned the handle and let them inside.

"Someone's impatient. The clock doesn't start until you've paid me, so you can chill." Josh sauntered in after him, flipping the lights on, and he made sure the door was locked on the inside.

Rupert didn't want to chill. He wanted Josh naked as soon as possible. "So, how does this work? Do you have ground rules?"

Josh pulled a strip of condoms and a few sachets of lube out of his pocket, tossed them on the bed, and then turned to face Rupert. "You give me cash up front, and if we go over the agreed time, you pay me the extra when we're done. I do the usual stuff: fucking and sucking. But always with condoms. I don't do BDSM, so if you want kink, you're with the wrong guy. I'm not tying you up and whipping you, and I definitely don't let anyone do that to me. That's not my bag. Vanilla sex only, but in any position you like, and I'm versatile." His gaze raked over Rupert, and he grinned knowingly. "But I'm guessing you want to top. Am I right?"

"Yeah." Rupert was more comfortable as a top generally, and Josh's cocky attitude made Rupert want to bend him over and fuck him into the middle of next week.

Josh spread his hands and shrugged. "So, are we doing this?"

"Yes." Spurred into action, Rupert got out his wallet and counted out the crisp new notes from the cash machine. "Here's two hundred." Handing the money to Josh made arousal surge through him again.

Josh checked the amount, then folded the notes and tucked them into the pocket of his jeans. He took a step closer and smiled, as though he knew exactly what effect this situation was having on Rupert.

"Okay. I'm yours for the next hour. What are you going to do with me?"

Rupert swallowed hard. He reached down to palm himself through his trousers and saw Josh follow the movement with his eyes. "I want you naked for starters."

Rupert took off his suit jacket and hung it on the back of a chair, and when he turned around, Josh was undressing. He didn't make a display of it, no sexy striptease, but somehow every movement was intensely erotic despite his lack of performance. The knowledge that he was baring himself for Rupert to touch, to taste, to fuck was almost more than he could stand. Josh kicked off his shoes first and then stripped off his T-shirt to reveal a long lean torso. The tattoo on his chest stood out starkly in indigo ink against his pale skin: two birds, their beaks almost touching on his sternum with their wing tips curling up to his collarbones. The rest of his skin looked unmarked, and he was mostly hairless, save for under his arms and a thin dark line that led from his navel below the waist of his black jeans.

Rupert focused his gaze on Josh's hands as he unbuckled and unzipped. Josh slid his jeans and underwear down in one unselfconscious move and his cock bobbed free, hard and flushed in a thatch of neatly trimmed pubes.

"Stupid skinny jeans," Josh muttered as he bent to free his feet, pulling his socks off at the same time. When he straightened up, he was beautifully, gloriously naked.

"You're gorgeous," Rupert said.

It was true. Josh had the body of a dancer, lithe and strong, but slender. He looked as though he would bend, but not break.

"Turn around, I want to see the arse I'm going to fuck."

For the first time Josh's cheeks flushed pink — with shame, or excitement? It was impossible to tell, but his cock was hard and straining upwards. Josh was clearly as turned on as Rupert was, so Rupert stayed in this unfamiliar role he was playing, keeping his face serious and waiting until Josh did as he asked.

Josh turned slowly and then looked at Rupert over his shoulder. "What do you think?"

"Perfect," Rupert murmured.

Wide shoulders tapered to a slim waist above high, tight buttocks. The skin of Josh's back was smooth, and a line of seven star tattoos marked the bumps of his spine, starting between his shoulders and ending just above the cleft of his arse. They decreased in size as they went.

Rupert moved up behind Josh and finally touched him again, kissing his neck and shoulders and gripping his hips so that he could push his clothed dick against that perfect arse.

Josh sighed and arched back into his touch. "You're so hard," he said. "Shall I suck you for a bit before you fuck me? I want to see your cock."

"Yeah," Rupert said, voice husky with want.

Josh turned and slid to his knees in front of him. He undid Rupert's fly with practised fingers and pulled his trousers and underwear down around his thighs. Rupert's cock stuck out obscenely between his shirttails, jerking as Josh grinned up at him.

"Nice," Josh said.

He wrapped his hand around Rupert's shaft and lifted it. Then he kissed Rupert's balls and licked up the underside of his shaft before reaching for a condom from the bed. The mere the action of him rolling it on had Rupert's breath hitching, and when Josh parted his lips and sucked Rupert down, the latex didn't take much away from the feeling of Josh's mouth around him. Maybe a little less sensation was a good thing, or Rupert might have struggled not to come from the wicked curl of Josh's tongue and the way he kept his eyes open to watch Rupert's every reaction as he sucked and licked.

Rupert slid his hands into Josh's silky hair and cupped his head. "That's good." He tried not to think about how many men Josh had done this for. It was ridiculous to feel so possessive about someone he hardly knew. Someone he was paying for.

He let Josh suck him until he was close, orgasm building at the base of his spine and in his balls, and then he gently pulled him off. "Can I fuck you now?"

"That's what we're here for." Josh got to his feet. "How do you want me?"

Rupert considered it for a moment. "On your front," he finally said. Rupert wanted to stay in control of this situation, and Josh's knowing expression was too much, as if he was aware of exactly what he was doing to Rupert and it amused him. Rupert wanted to be able to lose himself in Josh, in this experience. It would be easier if he couldn't see his face.

Josh crawled onto the bed. "Like this?" He waited on all fours, legs apart and arse on display.

Rupert bit back a groan at the sight. "Yes." He kicked out of his trousers and underwear but was too impatient to take off his shirt or socks. Moving to his knees behind Josh, Rupert held Josh's cheeks apart and stroked his thumb over Josh's hole. "Fuck," he muttered. "There's already some lube there."

"Just a little. I like to be prepared—*ahh*."

Josh's light drawl broke off into a gasp as Rupert pushed two fingers inside him where he was slick. He was still tight, though, clinging around Rupert's fingers and squeezing.

Rupert imagined Josh prepping himself earlier this evening, fingering his arse for some nameless, faceless man who would have paid Josh for this, just like Rupert had. He felt dizzy with the urge to be inside Josh, to fuck him, to possess him. But he wanted this to be good for Josh as well as him. If this was the only time he got to do this, he wanted to make an impression. He wanted Josh to remember him.

He curled his fingers, probing and thrusting carefully until he found what he was looking for. Josh gasped again, the muscles in his back going taut.

"You can fuck me now, you know. I don't need all this."

"But you like it." Josh didn't deny it, so Rupert stroked over that spot relentlessly. "I like making you feel good."

Josh was breathing hard, rocking back onto his fingers. Rupert reached between Josh's legs with his other hand and found his cock, hard and leaking.

"Rupert," Josh groaned. It was the first time he'd said Rupert's name. "I'm going to come on your fingers if you don't stop. Wouldn't you rather be inside me?"

Josh's voice was hoarse, all trace of his earlier cockiness gone, and the desperate edge finally stripped away the last of Rupert's patience. He dragged his fingers out, making Josh hiss at the loss, and ripped open a packet of lube. Then he smeared it liberally over his sheathed cock and wiped his hand on the sheets before gripping Josh's hip firmly with one hand and lining himself up with the other.

They moaned in unison as Rupert slid into the tight, grasping heat of Josh's body. He wasn't gentle or careful — he didn't need to be. Josh was demanding right from the start, pushing back against him and urging him on. "Yeah, come on. Fuck me."

"Are you this pushy with all your clients?" Rupert slammed in hard, knocking a cry out of Josh.

"Only if I think they'll like it. Fuck, yes. Do it like that."

The bed creaked and banged against the wall. Rupert wondered whether there was anyone next door, listening to the sounds of their coupling. The thought of it turned him on even more. He fucked Josh harder, leaning over him and trying to drag over Josh's prostate with every thrust. From the sounds Josh was making, he was pretty sure he was managing it.

"You gonna come for me?"

"I'm close, but I can't…."

Josh tried to get a hand underneath himself, but the force of Rupert's thrusts made him lose his balance. Rupert was using his grip on Josh's hips for leverage, so he couldn't help him out in this position. He pulled out and flipped Josh onto his back. Now Josh had stopped teasing, Rupert wanted to see what he was doing to him. Josh was a mess, face and neck flushed, and his lips bitten pink. His cock was rock hard and leaking onto his belly. Rupert felt a mad urge to lean down and suck it into his mouth, but he knew Josh would insist on a condom.

He held Josh's legs up and back, tilting his hips so he could push back into him. Josh's eyes flew wide as Rupert used the upward curve of his cock to devastating effect. Rupert leaned down to kiss Josh again, a dirty, hungry kiss that Josh returned enthusiastically. He felt the bump of Josh's hand against his stomach and realised Josh was stroking himself.

He kissed down Josh's neck, tasting his skin. "Yeah," he said, "make yourself come."

"Are you close too?" Josh's voice was tight and strained.

"Yeah." Rupert pushed himself up on his arms so that he could watch the frantic movement of Josh's hand. "I've been close ever since you sucked me."

Josh made a noise that sounded almost like a sob, and came all over himself, his arse squeezing tight around Rupert as he painted his belly with sticky stripes.

"Fuck," Rupert moaned, finally letting go and fucking into Josh with a last few desperate thrusts until he followed, dragged over the edge by the sight of Josh arching beneath him.

Rupert fell forward, and Josh made a small humming sound of satisfaction as he put his arms around him. Josh traced his fingers lightly over Rupert's back until Rupert's head stopped spinning and his heart rate was back to normal.

"Good?" Josh asked quietly.

"Mmm." Rupert nodded, his face still pressed into the curve of Josh's neck. Josh smelled good, of clean sweat and man.

Josh started to chuckle.

"What?" Rupert lifted his head to see Josh's grin.

"Your shirt. It's covered in spunk."

"Bollocks."

Rupert had been so far gone, he'd forgotten he still had his shirt on. He peeled himself off Josh, and sure enough, the pale blue material was sticky with Josh's come.

"You're going to be wearing me for the rest of the evening. Eau de Josh." The teasing tone was back.

"Good thing it's dark outside." Rupert flopped onto his back, pulled off the condom, and knotted it before throwing it into the bin. "Anyway. We're not done here yet. It'll dry."

"Yeah? You want more?" Josh rolled onto his side and propped his head up on his elbow. "Maybe you should take your shirt off for round two."

Josh's eyes had dark shadows under them, Rupert noticed now. A flicker of tenderness took him by surprise.

"Maybe in a little while." He put an arm around Josh and pulled him to lie with his head on Rupert's chest. "Is this okay?" he asked softly.

"Yeah. It's nice." Josh relaxed into him.

Rupert stroked his hair, holding him close until he felt Josh's body relax completely. He listened to his slow, steady breathing and realised Josh had fallen asleep.

Josh stirred and mumbled as Rupert extricated himself, but didn't wake. Rupert pulled his clothes on silently, not wanting to disturb him. Josh obviously needed the sleep. Once dressed, he scribbled a note on the hotel paper with the pen provided, tore the sheet off, and left it on the bedside table. He stood for a moment, watching Josh. Josh looked so vulnerable, so trusting. Feeling foolish, but unable to stop himself, Rupert stooped and pressed a light kiss to Josh's cheek.

"Sweet dreams."

## CHAPTER THREE

Josh woke slowly from the heavy sleep of the truly exhausted. He stretched, eyes still closed, and as the sheets slipped over bare skin, he realised he was naked. The second thing he registered was that he wasn't in his own bed.

*What the hell?*

He sat up, staring around the hotel room. Grey light filtered around the edges of the curtains, and the glowing red numbers on the digital clock by the bed told him it was just after five in the morning. He flopped back on the bed and rubbed his eyes as the events of the evening before took shape in his sleep-addled mind.

Philip hadn't shown... and then he'd met that other bloke... Rupert.

*Fuck.*

He must have fallen asleep on him. Bloody hell. Instinctively he rolled to grab his jeans from the floor and checked the pockets. His phone was still there, and the cash Rupert had given him. Then he spotted the note on the bedside table, written on hotel paper in a dark scrawl of ink.

*I didn't get your number before you crashed out. But I'd like to see you again. Text me?*

Rupert had signed his name and added his number at the bottom of the page.

Josh stared at the paper. The wording was ambiguous. But surely by "see," Rupert meant a booking?

Josh's body flushed at the memory of the night before. Rupert had been good in the sack, considerate and sexy as hell. Josh didn't always get off with his clients; not all of them cared whether he did or not. When Josh enjoyed the sex as much as they did, it was a bonus. He was always up for taking on new clients who were a good fuck, and he could always use more regulars to pay the bills.

He put Rupert's number into his phone and scrumpled up the note, chucking it in the bin along with the condom from the night before.

Josh couldn't get back to sleep in the hotel room, so he dressed and left.

He almost never spent a whole night with a client and it was unusual for him to do the walk of shame. The streets were deserted at this time of the morning. A gaggle of seagulls, all noisy squawks and flapping wings, fought over a discarded burger in the gutter. Bold with hunger and intent on their battle, they didn't react as Josh passed by.

When he got back to the house he shared with five other students, all was quiet. His housemates wouldn't be up for hours. Josh was wide awake now, so he made himself some coffee and toast, showered, and then holed up in his room to catch up on some studying. Maybe he'd manage to nap this afternoon. He had another client scheduled for tonight, and he really didn't want to fall asleep on two guys in as many days.

Rupert remained obstinately in Josh's head throughout the day. Every time his mind wandered from his books, he pictured red hair and clear blue eyes, and saw the expression on Rupert's face as he'd come.

Josh didn't usually daydream about his clients, but by lunchtime he gave up trying to push the images away and jerked off to them instead. He fingered himself as he did it, still sensitive from where Rupert's cock had stretched him open. If he had to bottom again tonight, Josh would still be feeling Rupert in his arse with every thrust.

Afterwards, he held his phone for a long time, staring at Rupert's contact details. *He's just a client. Just another client. But he's hot, and he'll pay you. What have you got to lose?*

Something in Josh was wary, but he sent the text anyway.

*Sorry I fell asleep on you. Josh.*

After he'd showered and washed away all traces of Rupert, Josh went downstairs. He heard two of his housemates, Shawn and Mike, arguing about something in the kitchen, so he headed into the living room where it was quieter.

Jez, Mac, and Dani were in there watching TV. They greeted him as he came in and he sat next to Dani on the sofa. Mac and Jez were sprawled on the other one in a tangle of limbs. Since they'd finally sorted their shit out and become a couple a few months ago, they'd been inseparable. Josh didn't begrudge them their obvious happiness, but sometimes seeing them together made him lonely.

Dani tucked up her feet to make room for him, and asked, "Are you okay? You were late last night."

She was the only one of his housemates who knew what his job was. He normally told her if he was planning on being out all night, so she wouldn't worry.

"I'm fine. Just stayed out longer than I'd planned. Sorry, Mum."

She poked him with her toes in protest, but the concern vanished from her features.

"Was he good, then?" Jez asked. "You must have shagged every bloke in Plymouth by now. You're the king of hook-ups — or should that be the queen?" He chuckled at his own joke.

As far as his male housemates were aware, Josh was out in bars or clubs on the nights he was working, and he was happy to let them believe that.

"Yeah, he was awesome," Josh said that to try and make Jez jealous. Although from the noises that came out of Jez's and Mac's rooms on a regular basis, Jez wasn't missing out on good sex by being in a monogamous relationship. Quite the opposite, in fact.

"You seeing him again?" Jez seemed more interested in Josh's non-existent love life than he was in the TV.

"Maybe. I got his number."

Dani caught Josh's eye and looked at him questioningly. He flushed.

Jez let the subject drop, and Josh was relieved. It wasn't that he was ashamed of what he did, but he didn't want to have to justify it. He'd only told Dani because she was his best friend and he trusted her completely. Plus she knew too much about his family not to be suspicious when he wasn't completely skint all the time. Josh's dad gave him nothing towards his living expenses, and Dani knew it.

Josh's client tonight was another regular, an older man who called himself Michael, but Josh suspected that wasn't his real name. Josh had been seeing him once a month for about a year, and the sex was always perfunctory. He got the impression that Michael's internalised homophobia was so extreme that he hated what they did as much as he got off on it. Michael turned up, fucked Josh in a way that was almost clinical, and left. No conversation beyond what was necessary, no connection, and no foreplay. Their appointments always left Josh unsatisfied, yet relieved he wasn't like Michael. Josh had never been ashamed of who he was.

Josh's phone rang as he was getting ready in his room. A glance at the screen showed Rupert's name, and he accepted the call straight away. "Hi," he said.

"Hi."

There was a pause.

"Did you want something?"

"I... uh. Yeah. Sorry. I wasn't sure you'd pick up."

"I sent you my number, didn't I?" Josh looked at his reflection in the mirror, combing his dark hair into place with his fingers while he spoke.

"So, can I see you again?"

The words came out in a rush. Rupert sounded nervous and on edge. Josh guessed he'd taken a while to work up to calling, and that made him smile.

"Sure. If you can afford me." Josh thought he'd make it clear that if he was seeing Rupert again, it would be a business transaction.

"Oh." A pause. "The money's not an issue. But I was hoping... never mind. Yeah. I can pay. When are you free?"

Josh mentally scanned his evening schedule. "Next Saturday?" He could have fitted Rupert in much sooner, but he needed breathing space before he saw him again. He didn't want to think about why.

"Okay."

"I'll text you about where and when nearer the time."

There was another pause, and Josh was about to bring the conversation to a close, when Rupert asked, "Did you sleep well... sleeping beauty?" He added the nickname as an afterthought, and Josh heard the gentle teasing in his tone. He flushed.

"Yeah... about that—"

"It's all right. You already apologised. I couldn't resist taking the piss a little. Do you do that with all your clients? I guess as long as it's after rather than during, then they wouldn't mind too much."

"Ha-ha," Josh said dryly. "But no. I've never done that before."

"Should I be insulted?" Rupert sounded more amused than annoyed.

"You should probably be flattered," Josh replied honestly. "Means I don't have you pegged as an axe murderer."

There was a soft chuckle on the other end of the line. "Okay. Flattered it is, then." Another pause. "Are you sure I can't just take you out for dinner on Saturday? Buy you a few drinks? You don't have to put out."

Rupert's voice was a little too casual for it to sound convincing. Josh's heart beat a little faster. Damn, he was tempted. He couldn't remember the last time he'd been on a date. It was easier not to bother. "Saturday's a work night for me," he hedged.

"A different night, then?"

Josh drew in a breath and let it out slowly. Could he? Could it work? At least Rupert already knew about his job and seemed okay with it.... But no. They'd started their relationship as escort and client. It was better to keep things simple.

"No, sorry. But I don't date. It's easier that way."

Rupert didn't seem surprised by Josh's answer. "Well, if you change your mind, I'm free most nights this week. Otherwise I'll see you Saturday."

"Okay. I'll text you. I have to go."

"Don't want to keep him waiting, huh?"

And the jealous edge to Rupert's tone was exactly why Josh knew he'd made the right decision. He could handle possessive clients, but the last thing he needed was a possessive boyfriend. That would make his life way too complicated.

"Yep. Bye, Rupert."

"Bye. Oh, and Josh?"

"Yeah?"

"Be careful."

"I always am."

Josh ended the call, not sure whether to feel irritated or touched by Rupert's concern.

With a sigh, Rupert put his phone down on the black leather arm of his sofa and ran a hand through his hair.

He hadn't expected Josh to agree to go on a date with him, but he could tell Josh had at least considered it. Rupert took that as a good sign. But mainly he was glad he was going to see Josh again, even if he had to pay for it. He'd been thinking about Josh all day. Perhaps another fuck would get Josh out of his system?

He considered going out for a drink, maybe even going out to a club and trying to pull, or getting online for another attempt at hooking up after his failure the night before — although it had worked out in his favour in the end, of course. It might be a good thing to remind himself that he could get sex without paying for it, but Rupert hated trying to pick up strangers. A natural introvert, the whole going out and charming people thing didn't come naturally to him. Also, the imprint of Josh still lingered in his memory. Rupert didn't think it would be easy to find someone who could erase that. He wasn't sure what it was about Josh that was so alluring. Was it a previously undiscovered kink for literally buying someone's body for a few hours, or was it more about Josh himself?

Sighing, Rupert reached for his laptop where it lay on the coffee table.

He groaned when he saw another email from his mother with "Wedding" in the subject line. The woman was relentless. She'd talked his ear off about her wedding plans last night, surely there couldn't be much else to say?

He started to read, and his blood pressure rose as he stared in disbelief at the words. He went back and reread. She couldn't seriously be suggesting....

She was.

"For fuck's sake!"

He considered his options. It wasn't as though he had a significant male other he wanted to bring. He'd been single for over a year now and wasn't going to take some random bloke to his mother's wedding. But was he really prepared to let his mother shove him back in the closet just to keep the peace with his homophobic soon-to-be stepfather?

Rupert had come out to his closest friends and family when he was sixteen. His mother had been outwardly accepting at the time, but mostly because of his dad's influence. Old sorrow tugged at Rupert's chest as he remembered how his dad had hugged him after Rupert got the words out. He'd told him he was proud of him and that he loved him. Then a few short months later, he was gone, taken from them in a waterskiing accident while on holiday in Cyprus.

Rupert had never explicitly told his mother's new partner, Charles, that he was gay. He assumed his mother must have told him, but it wasn't something that had ever come up in conversation on the few occasions he'd met Charles.

*It's only one day. Maybe it's worth it for a quiet life.*

He picked up his phone again, pulled up Georgina's number, and hit Call.

She answered after a few rings. "Hi, Rupert."

Her clipped, public school voice always sounded so much more precise on the phone than in person.

"Hi, how's things?"

"Same old, same old. Too much work and not enough hours in the day." Georgina worked in the media team at the university. They had met when Rupert had been called in to fix a network problem in her department, and they'd hit it off immediately. They'd been lunch and coffee-date friends ever since. "How's life with you?"

"Pretty good, thanks."

"So... what can I do for you?"

"Well, um, I was actually phoning to ask you a favour."

"Sounds ominous."

"I know this is rather short notice... but my mother's getting married on the last weekend in May. I need a plus-one for the wedding, and was wondering whether you were free to come with me?"

"Really, Rupert? I thought you were dating again. Don't you have a potential boyfriend you can take?"

"My mother wants me to bring a *nice girl*" — he emphasised the words to show they were his mother's rather than his own — "and I think you fit the bill."

"Why the hell did your mother specify a girl? She's never had a problem with you dating guys, has she?"

"Not that I knew of, no." Rupert sighed. "I think Charles, her fiancé, is the one with the stick up his arse. But I get the impression it'll make the big day go more smoothly if I don't rock the boat by turning up with a man, and I don't have a guy to ask anyway. So, can you come?"

There was the sound of movement on the other end. "I'm just checking my calendar... but honestly. I think your mother's attitude is awful.... Okay, yes, I'm free. But are you sure you want to do this?"

Rupert sighed. "Yes. It's just less hassle this way."

"You owe me big time for this."

"I know. It's bound to be massively tedious. All pomp and ceremony and speeches, and people asking me about my job, then asking for advice about their own computers when I tell them what I do. There won't even be a disco to sweeten the pill. Let's hope there's plenty of booze is all I can say."

"You don't have to put yourself through this, you know. Can't you fake an illness that weekend? A vomiting bug is always a great excuse."

"She'd never forgive me. She probably wouldn't believe me either. No. I'll have to get through it."

"I can't believe you're letting her push you into this. What happened to that boy you told me about who marched in all the pride parades when he was a student? He wouldn't take a woman as his plus-one just to keep his mother happy."

She had a point.

"It would be different if there was a guy I wanted to take. But there isn't," Rupert said.

"Are you still not even dating?"

"Not really." Rupert thought about his failed attempt at a date the night before, and that led his thoughts back to Josh again. The urge to talk about him was too strong to resist. "But I did meet someone last night."

"Ooh, tell me more! Did you meet him in the exchanging-phone-numbers sense, or the getting-naked sense? I want details. What's his name? What's he like? Are you seeing him again?"

Rupert laughed. "If I can get a word in, I'll tell you. I met him in a bar, and we hooked up. He's called Josh, and I'm seeing him again next weekend." Rupert was all too aware of the salient information missing from his summary, but no way was he going to tell Georgina the part where Josh was an escort.

"What does he look like?"

"He's hot. Lean and sexy, with dark hair and amazing green eyes. He's got tattoos and a lip ring."

"Not your usual type, then."

"I suppose not." In the past Rupert had always gone for conventional, wholesome-looking guys. Guys who looked more like himself. Josh was definitely a step out of his comfort zone with his slightly edgy look.

"And you like him?"

Rupert hesitated, and then admitted it. "Yeah. It was only one evening, but I like him."

"You should ask *him* to the wedding instead of me."

"I don't think so."

"Too soon? You don't want to scare him off?"

"Something like that. My mother's enough to scare anyone off," Rupert joked to cover the slight awkwardness. He regretted mentioning Josh now. It was stupid. Josh was never going to be boyfriend material, and Rupert needed to get that very clear in his head before he saw him again.

Georgina chuckled. "Your mother does sound as if she needs careful handling. Oh hell, look at the time. I'm sorry, but I have to go."

"Hot date?"

"Nothing very exciting. I'm meeting a girlfriend to go to the cinema, but I'll be late to meet her for drinks first if I don't get a move on. I've put the wedding on my calendar, but I still think you should ask your Josh. He can always say no."

"He's not *my* Josh." Rupert's stomach clenched as he remembered Josh was probably with another man right now.

"Whatever. Okay. Bye, Rupe. Let's meet for coffee soon. I'll text you."

"Yes. Bye."


As the week passed, Rupert got increasingly twitchy as he waited to hear from Josh.

He kept telling himself it was ridiculous to be stressing over it when Josh wasn't his date. This was a business transaction, for fuck's sake. It should be like waiting for a call from a plumber or an electrician. Josh wanted his money. He'd get in touch. But somehow that didn't help matters.

He found himself looking out for Josh around the university, hoping he might catch sight of him around campus. But he didn't.

Josh finally texted him on Friday afternoon.

*U still up for tomorrow evening? What time suits?*

Rupert's heart thumped as he replied.

*Yes. Anytime from 8pm.*

*Can we make it 9?*

*Sure. Where shall I meet you?*

*Same hotel. I'll text you the room number once I've booked.*

Damn. Rupert should have suggested a drink first, but it was too late now. He didn't want to appear too pushy.

*Okay, c u then,* he typed. Then added as an afterthought. *Make sure you get an early night tonight ;)*

*You're never going to let me live that down are you?* Josh replied.

*Nope.*

## CHAPTER FOUR

Josh had mixed feelings about his forthcoming appointment with Rupert.

On the one hand, he was looking forward to the sex. He was undeniably attracted to Rupert—he'd been a great fuck last weekend. But on the other hand, Rupert had been on his mind too much this week, and Josh wasn't comfortable with that.

The anticipation fizzed through him as he got ready to go and meet Rupert. He had to jerk off in the shower because just thinking about Rupert got him hard. Then after, when he fingered himself with a little lube in his room, one foot up on the desk, he got a semi again even though he'd only come ten minutes before.

Josh arrived at the hotel ten minutes early and tried to combat his jitters by taking control of the situation. He pulled the curtains and turned the lamps on, adjusting the dimmer switches until he was satisfied. He took off his shoes and socks and lay on the bed, trying to slow his breathing and relax, but it didn't work. So he got up and paced instead.

He hadn't been this nervous about meeting a client since the first appointment he'd booked through his website. What the hell was wrong with him?

The soft knock on the door made him jump like a startled cat. His heart sped up and didn't slow as he went to let Rupert in.

"Hi." Josh smiled seductively, putting on his best veneer of cocky confidence. He'd trained himself to never show his nerves in front of clients.

"Hi." Rupert's genuine smile disarmed Josh, sending his excitement fluttering and swirling in his belly like confetti in a breeze.

Josh stood aside to let him in, and when Rupert stepped close and kissed him on the lips, it felt like a greeting from a date, or even a lover. The kiss was slow and lingering, the promise of something more.

"Haven't you forgotten something?" Josh said teasingly when Rupert released him. "Money up front, remember."

Rupert's face remained carefully neutral as he pulled a wad of cash out of his pocket. "Here. For two hours this time."

"Cool, thanks." Josh made a show of counting the cash, even though his instincts told him he could trust Rupert.

When he was done, he shoved the money into his pocket and looked Rupert up and down. Rupert was dressed very differently to last weekend. The smart clothes were gone, replaced by soft blue jeans that hugged his muscular thighs, and a dark grey T-shirt. The messy red curls were the same, though; as was the stubble that Josh's fingers itched to touch.

"Do you approve?" Rupert's lips quirked into a grin.

Josh shrugged. "Not bad, I suppose." But he couldn't hide the smile that tugged at his lips too. "You look more like an IT guy tonight with the casual look. I'm not sure if that's a good thing or a bad thing. I kind of liked the suit."

"Oh yeah?" Rupert advanced on him, putting his hands on Josh's hips and tugging him close.

Josh's hum of agreement was muffled by Rupert's lips as he kissed him, a slow, deep kiss that sent a rush of heat through Josh, making his cock stiffen fast. He slid his hands up Rupert's broad back, feeling the muscles under his palms, and tugged him closer, licking deeper into his mouth. He smiled into the kiss when he felt the hardness of Rupert's cock against his own.

Josh moved his hips in a slow, dirty grind, murmuring against Rupert's skin. "You gonna fuck me again?" He kissed over his stubbled jaw and down to the smooth skin below his ear. "Stick your fat cock in me and make me come?"

"If you want me to." Rupert tilted his head back and let Josh nip and suck lightly at his neck. He moved his hips against Josh's in perfect counterpoint, sending jolts of sensation up Josh's spine as their cocks bumped and caught through the fabric of their jeans.

"This isn't about what *I* want, remember?" Josh said. "You get to choose."

Rupert took Josh's head between his hands and gently tugged him away from where he was kissing Rupert's neck, so that their gazes locked. His blue eyes were intense and serious, and Josh couldn't help but stare back.

"I choose what makes you feel good," Rupert said. "Just because I'm paying doesn't mean I don't want you to enjoy this too. I get off on you getting off. So I want you to tell me what you want... what feels good for you. I want you to be honest."

Josh swallowed and then nodded. "Okay." His voice came out as a hoarse whisper, so he cleared his throat. "Okay," he said more clearly. "Then I want you to fuck me again. That was great last time."

Rupert flushed, not hiding his pleasure at the words. "It was for me too."

They kissed again, slow and unhurried. Rupert peeled Josh's T-shirt off and kissed the ink on his chest, then dipped his head lower to lick Josh's nipples until they hardened under his tongue. Josh slid his hands under Rupert's shirt to find solid muscle and the soft tickle of body hair against his palms.

"Take yours off too," he said, pushing the fabric up.

Rupert smiled and obliged. Losing the shirt released the heady scent of his body, and Josh kissed his chest, nuzzling at the scratchy hair over his powerful pecs where his scent was strongest, before lifting his face to kiss Rupert's mouth again.

Rupert started on Josh's fly, so Josh got his hands down too and they unfastened each other's trousers with clumsy fingers. Josh pulled out Rupert's cock and stroked the silky hardness, and Rupert did the same for him, hands working in unison. Josh moaned into the kiss, all his nerves swept away by fast-building arousal. He bit back a sound of protest when Rupert stopped stroking his cock and reached around to grip his arse instead, but then Rupert slid his fingers into the crack and found where Josh was slick for him. He pushed the tips of two fingers inside easily and fucked them in and out making Josh push back, wanting them deeper.

"That good?" Rupert murmured, sliding his mouth along Josh's jaw, all hot breath and the delicious scratch of stubble where Josh was clean-shaven.

"Yeah," Josh managed. The relentless stab of Rupert's fingers took his breath away.

"You want more?"

Josh nodded, gasping as Rupert tugged on his rim then pushed a little deeper. Then Rupert's fingers were gone and he gripped Josh's hips with strong hands, turning him and pushing him towards the full-length mirror on the wall beside the bed. He manhandled Josh till he was standing, hips tilted, hands braced on the wall on either side of the mirror. "There." Rupert met Josh's eyes in the glass. "Where are the condoms?"

"In my pocket."

Rupert crouched down to where Josh's jeans had fallen below his knees. But he didn't straighten up immediately. "You have the most beautiful arse."

Warm breath brushed the arse in question, tickling and making Josh tense with expectation. Then Rupert kissed each cheek in turn, deliberately running his stubbled chin over the sensitive skin. Josh's legs wobbled, and he widened his stance as much as the trousers around his ankles would allow. A warm hand cupped his balls and squeezed.

Still on his knees, Rupert started fingering Josh again. He curled them in deep, sending a flicker of electric sensation through Josh as Rupert found his prostate and stroked it with each careful press of his fingers.

Josh stared at his own reflection. His pupils were huge, almost eclipsing the green, and his mouth was slack, lips livid pink from Rupert's stubble and rough kisses. Seeing himself like that, so undone by the movement of Rupert's fingers inside him, was too much. He dropped his gaze instead to where his cock bobbed, hard and aching, with precome beading at the slit. As he watched, the glistening drop overflowed and stretched into a strand before breaking and dropping onto the carpet beneath.

Just when Josh thought he might come from this, without Rupert even touching his dick, Rupert withdrew his fingers and stood. He pressed a kiss to the back of Josh's neck, his erection sliding up the crack of Josh's arse. Josh pushed back against it, desperate, needing it inside him. "Come *on*."

Rupert chuckled. "Give me a sec."

There was the tear of a condom wrapper and a few agonising seconds of no contact, and then Rupert was back, lining up and pushing inside in one long, perfect stroke, filling Josh until he gasped. Eyes wide, he caught Rupert's gaze over his shoulder again.

"Fuck, that's hot." Rupert gripped Josh's hips tightly as he drew back and thrust in again, hard, knocking the breath out of Josh in a moan. Josh braced himself, rocking back to meet it.

"Harder," he said, holding Rupert's gaze.

"Yeah?" Rupert slammed into him again.

Josh let his head drop, giving in to the sensation of Rupert fucking him, taking him apart with each deep thrust. His awareness narrowed down to the burn in his pelvis, the inevitable build of sensation like a wave gathering strength before it crashed on the shore. He made sounds he couldn't control, crying out with each drag of Rupert inside him. He felt the scrape and sting of teeth on his shoulder.

"Look at me," Rupert said.

Josh raised his head and sought out that blue gaze. Rupert looked how Josh felt, glassy and unfocused. As their gazes locked, Rupert reached around to grip Josh's cock. The force of his thrusts pushed Josh into his fist, the perfect grip and pressure almost too much to bear.

"*Fuck*," Josh moaned. His legs were shaking now.

"Yeah, come on."

Rupert stroked him faster, fucked him harder, and Josh came in a blinding rush, hitting the mirror with the first shot of come as he pulsed around Rupert. He forced his eyes to stay open, fixed on Rupert's as his orgasm overwhelmed him. He was dimly aware of Rupert pulling out, and he managed to keep himself upright as Rupert jerked himself off, the sound of his hand audible over their ragged breathing. Rupert must have stripped off the condom because when he came, it splashed hot over the small of Josh's back and trickled into the crack of his arse.

Afterwards Rupert guided Josh to the bed. Josh still had his trousers around his ankles, and his legs felt like overcooked spaghetti. He collapsed onto his back, not caring how sticky he was.

"I'll get a cloth," Rupert said.

"Thanks." Josh was way too fucked to move for a few minutes.

Feeling oddly vulnerable after the heat of the moment had passed, Josh kicked out of his jeans, rolled to his side, and got under the covers, facing away from the bathroom door. He heard Rupert come back and move around for a few minutes before the bed dipped and Rupert moved in behind Josh. Rupert slid his arm around Josh and pressed a kiss to his shoulder.

"Thought you were getting a cloth?"

"I did. For the carpet and the mirror." Rupert's voice was warm with amusement. "Thought you might get charged extra for the cleaning otherwise."

Josh chuckled. "Yeah, probably. Thought you'd get a cloth for me too, though."

"Nah. I like you covered in my come."

"Kinky."

Rupert hummed his agreement with another kiss, to the back of Josh's neck this time. Then he asked, "Do you always prep yourself first?"

"Usually. Why?"

"I want to do it next time."

"Is there going to be a next time?"

"I hope so."

Josh tried to tamp down the thrill of excitement that surged in his chest. "Okay." He turned in Rupert's arms, rearranging himself with a hand tucked under his head. Rupert's hand rested lightly on Josh's waist, a point of warm contact, his fingers circling idly.

"Next Saturday?" Rupert asked.

"I think I'm already booked." Rupert's face clouded, so Josh quickly added, "But I could do Friday."

"Okay." The displeasure didn't entirely lift from Rupert's expression, but he was making an effort to hide it.

"I'm surprised you can afford me three weeks in a row," Josh said lightly. "They must be paying you way too much in the IT department. I wouldn't have thought your salary would stretch to expensive rent boys." He said it to remind Rupert about the boundaries — or maybe to remind himself. Rupert only owned Josh for the hours he paid him. The rest of the time they were nothing to each other.

"It doesn't," Rupert replied.

"So what, did you rob a bank or something?"

Rupert laughed, but he didn't offer any more explanation, and Josh was left wondering how he could afford the prices Josh charged on a regular basis. He wasn't complaining, though. Most of his regulars were high-earning businessmen, but that meant they were often considerably older than Josh. It was a novelty to have more than one appointment with someone under thirty.

Josh frowned as he studied Rupert. He reckoned he was in his mid-twenties, or maybe a little older.

"What?" Rupert asked.

"I was just wondering how old you are."

"Twenty-six. What about you?"

"Twenty-two."

Rupert raised his eyebrows in surprise. "I thought you were younger. But I'm relieved to find you're not a teenager. I did wonder."

"I'm in my second year at uni, but I started late. I left school at sixteen. Went back to college a couple of years later to do my A levels."

"Oh yeah?"

Josh ignored the questioning tone. The less said about those two lost years of drinking and taking any drugs he could get his hands on, the better. He was lucky to have come through it without getting arrested or worse, and he wasn't proud of that part of his past. The memory of those dark days was what kept him focused now, working his way out of the shitty hand life had dealt him in order to secure himself a better future. It gave him the drive to work, to earn the money he needed, to succeed.

He could see Rupert looking at him speculatively, and, wanting to fend off any more questions, he moved closer until their lips were nearly touching. He reached down and cupped Rupert's soft cock. Squeezing lightly, he murmured, "Are we gonna talk for the rest of your time, or do you want to fuck me again?"

Rupert curled a hand around Josh's neck and kissed him. The kiss was deep and Josh's heart was pounding when Rupert pulled away and grinned. "In case it wasn't obvious, that's a yes to fucking again."

The second time was nothing like the first. Rupert rolled on top of Josh and snogged him senseless before moving down his body, trailing teasing kisses and licks over his torso. He nosed at the line of hair below Josh's navel and breathed warm air over his cock before pressing just one kiss to the shaft and moving south to lick at his balls.

Josh parted his thighs to give him space and groaned as Rupert sucked on the skin behind his balls, so close to where he wanted Rupert's mouth.

As though Rupert could read his mind—"God, I want to eat you out. But lube tastes gross."—he moved back up and nuzzled Josh's cock. "I want to suck you too, you smell so good."

Josh was about to tell him he could, with a condom, of course, but Rupert was already moving up to kiss him again. He stroked Josh until he was fully hard.

"What do you want?"

"Fuck me," Josh said between kisses. "Just fuck me."

When Rupert pushed into him, he kept kissing Josh, circling his hips and rocking in with perfect pressure. Josh moaned his approval and bucked up to meet him, begging for more with his body because his mouth was otherwise occupied.

But Rupert kept the pace maddeningly slow. Josh's cock was trapped between their bodies, getting some friction with each careful thrust, but it wasn't quite enough.

Josh felt Rupert's tempo gradually build, his breathing getting faster and the sounds he made between kisses becoming wilder. Josh was so close now, right on the edge.

"Can you come like this?" Rupert drew back to ask, jaw tight as he struggled for control.

"I don't know… but don't stop." It was too good, Josh was riding that crest, and he didn't care how long he stayed there. The destination was less important than the journey.

So Rupert carried on, and Josh lost himself in the sweet slide of Rupert's cock inside him and the hunger of his kisses. When Rupert came, Josh clenched around him, milking out his release, holding him tight as he shuddered and stilled.

"Sorry." Rupert smiled ruefully. "You feel too good. I couldn't hold out."

He eased himself out of Josh and slid down the bed. Before Josh realised what was happening, Rupert had Josh's cock in his mouth and was sucking lightly on the head.

"Oh God," Josh moaned, pushing half-heartedly at Rupert's head. "You shouldn't... not without a condom."

Rupert pulled away. "Do you test regularly?"

"Yes, but—"

"And you're negative?" His breath was a hot caress on the tip of Josh's cock, so tantalising.

"Yes."

"Me too."

There was a long pause, and then Josh's cock jerked involuntarily and tapped Rupert on the chin.

They both laughed.

"Okay," Josh said. "But I'll warn you when I'm going to come."

Rupert didn't waste any time, sucking Josh down into the silken heat of his mouth until Josh's toes curled with pleasure so deep, he knew this wouldn't take long. It felt like forever since he'd had another guy's mouth on him without a barrier, and it was so damn good. He started to move his hips, unable to stop himself from thrusting up into that delicious, wet, warmth. Rupert hummed around him, encouraging him. Then Josh felt Rupert's fingers circling his hole.

"Yeah," he gasped. "Yeah, do it."

Rupert's fingers were dry, and Josh was sensitive from being fucked. It was almost too much but the curl and press was exactly what he needed. Lightning exploded up his spine and his hips bucked. "I'm gonna come," he warned Rupert.

Rupert pulled off just in time but carried on fucking Josh with his fingers. Come shot out of Josh's cock in thick sticky strands as his body locked tight, muscles straining. Josh groaned, then hissed as it became too much, wriggling away from those relentless fingers.

"You done?" Rupert grinned up at him.

"Fuck. Yeah," Josh managed weakly, "you could say that. Jesus."

Rupert chuckled softly and crawled up the bed to press a soft kiss to Josh's lips before collapsing back beside him. "Come here." He lifted his arm, encouraging Josh into his embrace.

Josh put his head on Rupert's chest. He lost track of how long they lay like that, with the thud of Rupert's heart a reassuring beat in Josh's ear. He was awake but relaxed, enjoying the feel of Rupert's arms around him.

Rupert finally broke the silence by asking, "How long have I got?" and Josh remembered they were on the clock.

"Dunno," he said. "I forgot to check the time when we started. It doesn't matter. I don't have anything else to do tonight, so I'm not in a hurry."

"Well, I'm not going to get it up again," Rupert said, amusement in his voice. "So don't hang around on my account." But he tightened his arms around Josh, and Josh stayed for a while. Fucked out and sleepy, he was in no rush to move.

## CHAPTER FIVE

When they finalised their arrangements for Friday, Rupert asked Josh to meet him for a drink first. "As part of the two hours," he'd assured Josh on the phone.

Josh agreed, so they met in the bar where Josh had picked him up exactly two weeks before.

Rupert arrived early and nursed a whisky and water while he waited for Josh to show. The anticipation bubbling inside made him feel as though he was on a date. He had to keep reminding himself that wasn't what this was. But his heart didn't get the memo, and it pounded erratically as Josh walked through the door a few minutes after nine.

"Sorry I'm late." He took the seat opposite Rupert. "I had to wait ages for a turn in the shower. The curse of living in shared houses."

He was flushed and breathless as though he'd been rushing. It reminded Rupert of how he looked in bed and did nothing to quell the excitement rippling through him.

"No worries, can I get you a drink?"

"Thanks, I'll have a lime and soda."

"Your usual?" Rupert's lips quirked, remembering that was what Josh had been drinking the first time they'd met.

Josh smiled. "I suppose."

Rupert had to wait a while at the bar to be served. He drummed his fingers impatiently, aware of the time ticking away while he was here instead of with Josh. Maybe they should have met in the hotel room again, but Rupert wanted more than a quick fuck. He caught sight of his reflection in the mirror behind the bar. He looked good, he thought objectively. He'd picked his clothes carefully tonight: a crisp white shirt that showed off the breadth of his shoulders and trim waist, paired with his best jeans.

He felt suddenly foolish for making the effort to look good for someone he didn't need to impress. Josh was a sure thing because Rupert was paying him.

Rupert had spent all week thinking way too much about Josh. He knew he should have been sensible and cancelled, made his excuses, and relegated Josh to a wank fantasy. It was crazy to keep paying someone for sex, to keep craving intimacy with someone he couldn't have—not the way Rupert wanted him. But the urge to see Josh again had been too strong.

"What can I get you?" The barman's words pulled Rupert out of his discomfiting thoughts. He ordered Josh's drink and carried it back to the table.

Josh's smile was welcoming, and he slid over on the bench seat, patting the space beside him, encouraging Rupert to sit there.

"Cheers." Josh raised his glass.

Rupert clinked his own against it before taking a sip of the bitter whisky.

"Don't you ever drink while you're with… while you're working?" Rupert tried to make light of it, but the words stuck in his throat. Again, he wondered what he was doing here and why he was doing this to himself.

"I don't drink at all." Josh didn't volunteer any more information, and the closed expression on his face discouraged Rupert from asking why.

"So, what do you do in your free time?" he asked instead, trying to get the conversation flowing. "Do you have time for hobbies?"

"Not much," Josh said. "Studying takes up most of my spare time, but I read to relax, or watch films, sometimes play computer games. I swim too — to keep fit."

"Indoors? Or in the sea?"

"Both. But indoors in the winter. I'm not one of those mad people who swim in the sea all year round. Have you seen them? There are some people who swim in the middle of winter." Josh mock shivered at the thought of it. "They don't even wear wetsuits."

Rupert chuckled. "Ouch."

"Yeah. I use the university pool in the colder weather, but I love swimming in the sea when it's warm enough."

The awkwardness from before had dissipated. Josh was animated and smiling, and seeing him like that made Rupert feel warm inside. Their knees brushed where Josh had angled himself to face Rupert, and the small point of contact was tantalising. Rupert wanted to touch him all over.

*Soon.*

While they finished their drinks, Rupert answered Josh's questions about his own hobbies. They both liked reading, although Rupert was more into contemporary fiction whereas Josh liked sci-fi and mysteries. There was more crossover in movie tastes, though they both liked quite a range.

The slightly halting conversation gradually became easier as they relaxed and opened up, and it felt like they were on a date. The subtle flirtation of extended eye contact and the warm pressure where their legs touched made Rupert's nerves and excitement build as they got closer to the time where they would take this somewhere private.

Josh was fiddling with a beer mat, tearing strips off it with his slender fingers, and Rupert's eyes kept getting drawn to the movement. He wondered if Josh was nervous too and whether this was his way of channelling it.

When both their glasses were empty, Rupert finally gave in to the urge to reach for Josh. He took Josh's hand and laced their fingers together. Squeezing gently, he asked, "Do you want to get out of here?"

As though Josh's answer wasn't already a foregone conclusion.

Josh paused for a beat, biting his lower lip, before going along with it. "Yeah, let's do that."

Rupert kept hold of Josh's hand as they wove their way between the tables. Josh didn't try to pull away, and Rupert felt the thrill of possession as he noticed a few people glancing their way and noticing their joined hands. The idea they might assume Josh was his boyfriend made Rupert's stomach flip, shocked by how much he wanted that. Once again he found himself wondering what the hell he was playing at.

Once they were alone in the hotel lift, Josh reeled him in and kissed him passionately, erasing all Rupert's misgivings. Josh threw his head back as Rupert kissed down his neck, and rode the thigh that Rupert shoved between his legs.

"Fuck, yes." Josh wound his fingers into Rupert's curls and tugged him back up to his mouth.

Distracted, they almost missed the lift stopping on their floor. Rupert was glad nobody was waiting to get in, because they couldn't keep their hands off each other as they stumbled down the corridor to the room Josh had booked.

They stripped as soon as they'd locked the door behind them. Josh seemed as impatient as Rupert was to touch and taste, and when Josh pulled down his underwear along with his jeans, his cock was hard and ready. Rupert was glad of the visible evidence of Josh's arousal, reassured that Josh wanted him too. He pulled Josh into his arms for another hungry kiss. Their erections bumped together, and Rupert took them both in one hand to squeeze and stroke for a moment. With his other hand, he reached around to cup Josh's arse, and Josh moaned into the kiss, pressing his cock into Rupert's grip so that they slid together.

Rupert pulled away. "Get on the bed." He slapped Josh's arse lightly as he moved. "No, on your stomach."

Josh complied, lying on his belly, head cradled on his arms. He spread his legs and tilted his hips invitingly.

Rupert's cock jerked as the sight of Josh's hole—tight and pink, waiting to be opened. He crawled onto the bed and lowered himself over Josh to kiss his neck first, and then his shoulders. He started with the inked star at the top of Josh's spine, and licked and sucked his way down to the smallest one that lay between the dimples at the bottom of his back. Rupert dragged his face deliberately over the smooth skin, tickling Josh with his stubble and making him squirm before moving lower still. He kissed the pale curves of Josh's buttocks, then took one in each hand and opened him up.

"Did you prep yourself today?" he asked.

"No," Josh answered breathlessly. "You said not to."

"Good." Rupert pressed his face into Josh's crack and licked a long, slow stroke from his taint up to the star at the base of his spine. Josh gasped as Rupert's tongue dragged over his hole and the muscle clenched and released. "Is this okay?" Rupert asked.

"Yeah." Josh's voice was strained.

Rupert licked again. This time he stopped at Josh's hole and lavished his attention there, circling his tongue and making him wet and slippery. Josh was clean from his shower but the tang of his body was there under the soap. Masculine and musky, it made Rupert's cock ache as it rubbed against the sheets. Josh started cursing, pushing back against Rupert's tongue and making little breathy moans of approval. His body softened, opening up, and Rupert pressed his tongue in, stabbing it into the muscle in sharp jabs that made Josh gasp. Josh spread his legs wider, rocking his hips rhythmically as he ground his cock against the bed.

"You're gonna make me come if you don't stop." His voice was hoarse, desperate.

Rupert didn't stop. He dug his fingers into Josh's arsecheeks and tongued him harder, humming encouragement until Josh stilled and came, his hole pulsing around Rupert's tongue as he shot his load into the sheets. "Oh… fuck. God that's…. *Fuck*."

Rupert never found out what it was, but he assumed it was good if Josh was having trouble getting the words out. He finally pulled away and wiped his face with the back of his hand.

"Okay?" He moved up to lie beside Josh, who seemed barely capable of moving, but managed to flop over onto his back and smile blearily at Rupert.

"Death by amazing orgasm," Josh chuckled. He looked drunk or high, pupils blown wide and cheeks flushed pink. He glanced down Rupert's body to his cock. "Give me a few minutes and I'll fuck you, or blow you. What do you want?"

"No rush," Rupert said, although he wasn't sure his cock agreed. He rolled closer for a kiss. That would do for now.

They kissed lazily for a while, Rupert trying to be patient while Josh came back to life. He ended up on top of Josh, rubbing off against his stomach in a slow, steady grind, smearing his precome into the smooth skin as he kissed Josh's neck. He was sensitive there, shivering and moaning with every slide of Rupert's tongue, every scrape of his stubble. Rupert sucked a little too hard and left a red mark at the juncture of Josh's neck and shoulder. He drew back and pressed his fingers against it. "Oops, sorry."

"I don't care." Josh tugged Rupert's head back down and tilted his own head back against the pillows in an invitation.

It was too tempting to resist, but Rupert avoided leaving marks high on Josh's neck. Josh might say he didn't care, but maybe he'd like the option to hide them at least. He wouldn't be able to hide them from whomever he was seeing tomorrow night, though—unless he kept his clothes on. That realisation sent a possessive surge through Rupert, making him suck harder, holding Josh's skin between his teeth as he drew the blood to the surface to mark his territory. He worked his way down Josh's torso, his kisses turning softer again. When he reached Josh's cock, it was half-hard, and Rupert drew it into his mouth and sucked until Josh was fully erect. Josh made no move to stop him this time, stroking Rupert's face as he sucked. After a few minutes, he pushed Rupert's hair out of his eyes and said, "I'm ready to go again. Want me to ride you?"

Rupert nodded, mouth still full of cock, and then he pulled off to grin and say, "Hell, yes."

They swapped positions. Rupert stretched out on his back, and Josh straddled him. Josh reached for the lube, but Rupert took it from his hand. "Let me."

He slicked his fingers and found Josh's hole, still soft and wet from Rupert's tongue. Two fingers went in easily, and Josh moaned, arching back into the sensation. Rupert thrust them gently, watching Josh for any sign of discomfort, but all he could see on his face was pleasure. Josh's cock jutted towards Rupert, bobbing slightly as he moved.

"Feels good." Josh said, eyes closed, and he raised himself up and sank back on Rupert's fingers, clenching around them and ratcheting Rupert's arousal up sharply.

Suddenly desperate to get inside that tight heat, Rupert muttered, "Condom?"

Josh moved to reach for one from the bedside table, his body twisting gracefully and those internal muscles tightening again as Rupert's fingers slipped free. Josh ripped it open and rolled it down Rupert's shaft in a practised move, then repositioned himself with the tip of Rupert's cock pressing against his hole. He sank back onto it. Rupert gasped as he felt tight, hot pressure around his crown, and then Josh eased himself all the way down.

"Fuck," Rupert hissed, gritting his teeth as he fought for control. "I won't last long."

"I'll go slow." Josh grinned down at him. Completely in control, he started jacking himself, just sitting on Rupert's dick. The only thing moving was his hand. Rupert watched the slide of it, up and down, the head peeking through his fist on each stroke. Occasionally Josh's internal muscles would squeeze reflexively, gripping Rupert's cock and making him try to push up and get some more friction, but Josh didn't budge until Rupert groaned.

"You want more?"

"There's slow, and then there's stationary. You can move a little. I think I can handle it."

Josh chuckled. But he started to move, a slow, dirty roll of his hips. "Oh fuck, that's good." He stroked himself faster and angled his hips slightly differently, squeezing hard around Rupert each time he rose before thrusting back down.

"Yeah?" Rupert had his hands on Josh's hips, not guiding, just feeling the movement of his muscles as he worked himself on Rupert's cock, taking his pleasure. Josh was definitely in the driving seat.

Josh grunted his agreement, his breathing coming fast now. He fucked down harder, the muscles in his thighs and belly flexing.

"You getting close?" Rupert really hoped he was, because he knew he wasn't going to be able to hold out much longer, not with these visuals and the way Josh felt around his cock.

"Uh-huh." Josh's face and neck were flushed, the red marks that Rupert had put there still livid. "Oh fuck... yes.... Fuck me *hard*."

Rupert took that as the signal to finally give in to the tension coiled tight in his balls. He gripped Josh's hips tightly and thrust up, hammering into him. Josh was right there with him as Rupert started to come. He stilled, buried deep inside Josh, and Josh came too, thick and sticky over his fist. There wasn't so much of it this time, but he carried on tensing and shuddering as he squeezed out the last few drops.

After they'd cleaned up, they lay on the bed in an embrace that felt so natural, it was difficult for Rupert to remember they weren't lovers — not in the normal sense of the word. He lay behind Josh with the covers pulled up to their waists. They were both still naked, and Rupert's lips brushed Josh's nape as he murmured into Josh's skin, "I don't want to move yet. Do you have to be anywhere, or can I pay you for an extra hour?"

"An extra hour's fine with me. Do you think you can get it up again?" His voice was teasing, but gentle.

"I don't care if I can't." Rupert wrapped an arm around Josh's waist and buried his nose in his hair. He was happy to pay Josh just for this. "I think you're addictive."

Josh laughed softly. "I'm an expensive habit to form."

"Good thing my father left me a healthy lump sum when he died, then." Rupert tried to sound flippant, but the words stuck in his throat.

Josh was silent. Rupert could feel the tension in his body.

"When did he die?" Josh asked.

"Years ago. When I was sixteen." Rupert braced himself for the inevitable *I'm sorry* that he'd heard so many times.

But instead Josh asked, "Were you close?"

"Yes." Rupert couldn't have elaborated around the lump in his throat even if he'd wanted to say more.

Maybe Josh heard the catch in his voice, because he turned in Rupert's embrace and wrapped his arms around him, holding him tight. "That sucks."

His easy affection unlocked something in Rupert, and he huffed out a half laugh, half sob, the sound muffled against Josh's shoulder. "Yep."

Josh didn't offer any other words of commiseration and didn't ask for details. But somehow, when Rupert got his emotions under control again, he found himself speaking anyway.

"We always got on well. He was very different to me…. Well, maybe not completely different. We're both focused, but in different ways. My father was a self-made man, came from very little. He bought and sold companies, made clever investments. He was good at what he did and made a lot of money. But he was good man, a good father. He never insisted I follow in his footsteps, and he was happy for me to follow my interest in computers. He expected me to work hard and do well at school, but he didn't try to shape me into a miniature version of himself."

Rupert paused and rolled away from Josh a little, looking at the ceiling as he spoke. The air was cool on his face after the warmth of Josh's skin. Josh kept his hand on Rupert's chest, his fingers stroking through the light fuzz of hair.

Prompted by the intimacy of what he'd just shared, Rupert blurted out the question he'd wanted to ask Josh since their first meeting.

"Josh, can I ask... why do you do this? I mean, I know you need to earn money. But why *this* job?"

He felt Josh tense, his fingers stilling for a fraction of a second before moving again.

"It's the best-paid job I could get that fits around my studies, simple as that. I like sex, so it's not a hardship."

"But you could get loans. Other students manage."

"I could. But why leave university thousands of pounds in debt if I don't need to? I don't get a penny from my dad, so I'd need loans for everything: fees, rent, living expenses. This way I can support myself and come out debt-free at the other end. I'm not ashamed of what I do, and it's my choice."

There was a finality to his tone that told Rupert the discussion was over as far as Josh was concerned. So he changed tack. "How come your dad doesn't help you?"

Josh snorted and turned onto his back, taking his hand away so that they were no longer touching. He paused so long before answering that

Rupert thought he wasn't going to reply at all. But then he said, "My dad's a total loser."

Rupert waited, and Josh elaborated. "He spends most of his time pissed, or high, or both. Well... I assume he still does, because I haven't seen him for two years."

"What about the rest of your family?"

"What family?" Josh said wryly. "My mum died of an overdose when I was small, and I don't have any siblings—thank God. Otherwise I'd probably have them to look after because I wouldn't trust my dad to look after a cat."

"Grandparents?"

"Dunno. If they're still alive, they never visited while I still lived at home. So there you have it, my sob story." Josh propped himself up on one elbow and glared at Rupert defensively. "But you don't need to feel sorry for me. I'm doing just fine. I've got a life plan and I'm sticking to it. Work, study hard, leave uni with a decent degree, and find a different job eventually. In the meantime, this works for me."

"Good for you, then," Rupert said, and he meant it. He was honestly impressed by Josh's resilience and determination. But he wondered where dating and relationships fitted into Josh's plan. He guessed they were filed away under "maybe in the future" along with the different job.

When Rupert's time with Josh was over, he got up and dressed reluctantly. Josh was sitting on the edge of the bed pulling on his socks when Rupert was ready to go.

"Thanks," Rupert said.

"You're welcome." Josh's lips curved. Rupert couldn't decide whether he was teasing or not.

"I'd like to see you again… for another appointment."

"Sure."

Josh stood, and Rupert moved closer. Without thinking too much about what he was doing, he cupped Josh's jaw with one hand and pressed a soft kiss to his lips. "I'll text you."

When he pulled back, Josh licked his lips. "Okay."

## CHAPTER SIX

When Rupert texted to arrange a midweek appointment, Josh agreed to see him on Wednesday night. He didn't have another client booked till Friday, when he was seeing Philip again.

They met in the usual hotel and, as always, the sex was good. Rupert found the fading marks on Josh's neck and sucked them back to the surface as he fucked him. He traced the red blotches with his fingers as they lay in a sweaty, postcoital heap in the ruined bed.

"Maybe you should piss on me instead," Josh teased.

"Huh?" Rupert's eyebrows shot up, and then he flushed with guilty realisation. "Yeah… maybe I should."

Josh grinned, his suspicions confirmed. "The guy I saw on Saturday commented on them."

"Good." Rupert's cheeks flushed as he admitted in a rush, "I hate to think of you with anyone else."

His possessiveness was a turn-on, so Josh played up to it. He moved to straddle Rupert, sliding his hands into his hair and kissing along the pale copper stubble that dusted his jaw.

"Does it help if I tell you that I think of you while they fuck me?" It was true enough. Josh had found Rupert sneaking into his fantasies while he was trying to come for the guy on Saturday. "That I wish it was your cock in my arse, your hand on my dick...."

The sharp catch of Rupert's breath told Josh he liked what Josh was saying. Rupert gripped Josh's arse and pulled him closer so that their hardening cocks rubbed together.

"But how do I know it's true? How do I know you're not just telling me what I want to hear?"

"Come on, Rupert. You can see how much you turn me on. The other guys are good, but I've already done stuff with you that I won't let them do. You sucked my cock without a rubber, remember? You rimmed me. I haven't had anyone else do that in ages. It's different with you."

And yes, Josh knew this *was* what Rupert wanted to hear, but it was all true. He meant every word. "Feel how hard you make me." He gasped as Rupert curled his fingers around Josh's erection.

Josh came like that, fucking into Rupert's fist while Rupert stroked him through it. Then Rupert jerked himself off afterwards while Josh murmured words of dirty encouragement between kisses.

Later, Rupert failed to hide his obvious displeasure when Josh said he couldn't see him on Friday, but he settled for Saturday instead. Josh kissed away the pout to his lips until he stopped frowning and smiled again.

Lying in bed on Saturday after they'd fucked, Rupert asked Josh if he could book all three of the nights Josh had scheduled as client nights in the following week.

"Seriously?" Josh turned so he could see Rupert's face.

Rupert flushed and avoided his gaze by looking at the calendar on his phone instead. "Is that a no?"

"No, it's not a no. But why, Rupert? Why spend all that money for sex with me? I mean… I know I'm good." He let a little humour creep into his voice. "But I'm not *that* good."

"Will you do it or not?" Rupert glanced at him then, his jaw set as he waited for Josh to reply.

Josh knew he should say no. Rupert was so far under his skin already that it wasn't a good idea to keep seeing him so frequently. If Josh were smart, he'd claim he had other bookings he couldn't get out of. He was already seeing Rupert more than he was comfortable with. Plus he felt oddly protective too. Whatever Rupert's motivations were, Josh was sure it wasn't wise for either of them to get tied into some weird, exclusive client-prostitute relationship. It couldn't last, and he didn't see any way it could end well.

But against his better judgement, he found himself agreeing. "Okay, then."

He could cancel the new guy he'd agreed to see on Friday. *Better to keep an existing client happy.* The smile that lit up Rupert's face sent a warm flush of answering pleasure and excitement through Josh. He tamped it down fast, but it did nothing to dispel his misgivings that he was biting off more than he could chew.

Each of the next three appointments went by much like their others.

They met for a drink first and exchanged small talk. It felt more like a date every time, and Josh had to keep reminding himself that wasn't what this was. They might act like lovers, but this was a job.

Rupert seemed to struggle with the boundaries too. He was affectionate in public, touching Josh's hand across the table, placing his palm in the small of Josh's back to guide him into the lift. But Josh wondered if that was part of the fantasy for Rupert, if he liked to imagine there was more between them than a verbal contract and an hourly rate.

After they'd come for the second time on Saturday night, they lay spooned together on top of the hotel covers. Josh had his back to Rupert. Rupert hadn't moved after fucking him other than to pull out and throw the condom into the bin. His arm was heavy and warm over Josh's ribs, and Josh was sleepy and comfortable. He knew the two hours Rupert had paid for had probably passed, but he didn't want to move.

"Can I book you for three nights next week too?" Rupert asked.

"I've got exams starting next week, so I'm taking a couple of weeks off."

"Oh... okay. Of course." There was an almost-hurt tone to Rupert's voice.

Josh put his hand over Rupert's where it rested on his stomach and let his fingers slide between Rupert's. "Sorry."

Rupert took his hand away and rolled to sit up. "No need to apologise. Your studies should come before your job. I understand." He sounded stiff and formal. "I'd better get going. I think my time's up for tonight." He got up and started gathering his clothes from where they'd been discarded in haste earlier. He kept his back to Josh as he stepped into his boxers and pulled them up.

Josh suddenly realised the prospect of two weeks without seeing Rupert wasn't very appealing to him either. He enjoyed the time they spent together—more than he should. "If I get a free night where I need a break from revising, I could call you," he offered. "If you wanted?"

Rupert straightened up and turned with a pleased smile. "Yeah. That would be good."

When he was dressed, he kissed Josh goodbye again as was his habit now. Today the kiss was a little more lingering than usual and when Rupert pulled away, he kept his hands on Josh's face for a moment.

"Good luck with the exams." There was a tenderness his expression that left Josh feeling slightly winded.

"Thanks," he managed. "See you in a couple of weeks... if not before."


During his first week of exams, Josh was too focused on revising to consider meeting Rupert, but they kept in touch by text. It started with a good-luck message on the morning of his first exam. Josh was touched that Rupert had remembered the date. Josh replied to say thanks, and then it developed into a text exchange that went on all week. Josh reported in to let him know how his exams had gone, and Rupert reminded him to take some breaks to sleep or eat.

On Thursday night Josh was taking a break from cramming for the exams he had the next morning. He and Dani were sprawled on the sofa, watching a film and sharing a bowl of popcorn. Josh's phone kept chiming with messages from Rupert. Rupert was asking for advice about what to get his mother for a wedding present — she was getting remarried soon, apparently — and Rupert had no clue what to get for the couple that already had everything. So far all Josh's suggestions had been rejected. The most recent one had been a hot-air balloon ride for two.

*Nope. She's scared of heights.*

*What about a painting or sculpture or something?* Josh typed and hit Send.

*Oh, that might work.*

*There's some cool glass sculptures at the arts centre at the moment. Maybe check them out?*

"Who is it you keep texting?" Dani asked.

"Just a client. Trying to sort out a time."

Josh's phone flashed up with a new message.

*I'm bad at choosing stuff like that though.*

*Well, get an arty friend to help.*

*Sounds like you know what you're talking about. I've never even been to the arts centre apart from to eat in the cafe there. Don't suppose you'd come and help me choose?* Then a few seconds later. *I'll buy you lunch there on Saturday if you're up for it.*

Josh paused, his thumb hovering over the keyboard. He couldn't ignore the lift of his spirits at the prospect of spending some time with Rupert. But what Rupert was suggesting sounded rather like a date.

"Fuck it," he muttered as he sent back a quick *OK*.

Rupert replied immediately with a smiley face that made Josh break into a grin he couldn't control.

"Texting clients to fix dates and times doesn't usually make you smile like that." Dani raised her eyebrows and her look was sceptical.

Josh flushed guiltily. "He is a client," he insisted. "It's just a bit...." He trailed off, unable to think of any word to complete the sentence other than *complicated*, and how lame was that—even if it was true. "I don't want to talk about it."

Of course that was the worst possible thing to say. Dani snatched up the remote and switched the TV off, then turned to sit cross-legged on the sofa, facing him. "Not wanting to talk usually means you *should* talk about it. So come on"—she poked his thigh—"spill!"

"Ugh." Josh ran his hands through his hair before moving to mirror her position, bracing his hands on his knees as he tried to work out how to explain the situation.

"Okay. It's this guy called Rupert. He's a client. I've been seeing him for about a month, regularly, and the lines have got a little blurry. But I'm not sure how to handle it."

"Blurry how?"

"I see him more often than anyone else, and it feels different with him. He always wants to go for a drink before... and he's never in a hurry to leave after. He's very affectionate. I don't know. Sometimes I have to remind myself he's only a client, not... more."

"Do you want it to be more?" Dani's voice was soft and careful.

Josh picked at his fingernails, unable to meet her gaze. He was afraid of what he'd see in her expression. He felt stupid and angry with himself for letting his feelings get out of control.

"No." It came out sharply. Maybe if he said it forcefully enough, he could convince himself. "I don't have time for a relationship, and anyway, it's too late. He's paying me to fuck him. That's not a good starting point for anything more meaningful, is it?" His attempt to make it sound like a joke fell flat, and the words came out sounding more bitter than he'd intended.

"Maybe you should stop seeing him if it's messing with your head?" she suggested.

"Yeah, perhaps. It's good money, though. Regular client, easy job. Getting paid to fuck someone who's hot and good in bed? I'm living the dream."

He snorted, managing to sound more convincing that time. He finally met Dani's eyes, but she wasn't smiling. She frowned, thoughtful and concerned.

"Just be careful, Josh."

"I always am."

There was an awkward silence. Josh was full of nervous energy now. Rather than reassuring him or helping him find a solution, the conversation with Dani had thrown all the things he'd been trying not to think about into the spotlight.

"I need some exercise," he said, unfolding himself from the sofa and stretching. "I'm gonna go for a swim."

On Saturday morning Josh was ridiculously nervous. He almost texted Rupert several times to cancel, but each time he hadn't been able to press Send. He knew right down to his bones that this was a bad idea, but he didn't care. The overriding desire to see Rupert wiped out all his instincts for self-preservation.

Josh had spent almost four years only doing things he needed to do. He'd worked every spare hour in crappy jobs and studied late into the night in order to put himself through college and finally get the grades he needed to go to uni. Then he'd started working as an escort as a means to an end. All his focus had been on escaping his background and earning himself the future he craved: a job that paid decent money, independence, choices. Those things were the bright shining light at the end of the tunnel, and Josh had been prepared to make any sacrifice necessary to get there. One of the sacrifices had been the possibility of a relationship. Until he met Rupert, that had seemed like a small price to pay.

Josh wasn't stupid. He knew this wasn't a real date. But it was something different to what he usually allowed himself, and he was going to take it.

It was a glorious sunny afternoon as he left the house to meet Rupert. The sky was the deep, perfect blue of early summer with just a few puffy white clouds. Warm, but not too hot. Josh's spirits rose like the seagulls riding the air currents above him as he walked.

He spotted Rupert waiting outside the Arts Centre for him, and his heart did a happy little skip as Rupert smiled and raised a hand to greet him. When Josh reached him, Rupert drew him into a hug and brushed a swift kiss over his cheek.

"Hi." Rupert looked as awkward as Josh felt, and that was oddly reassuring.

"Hi." Josh's cheek still tingled where Rupert's soft lips and rough stubble had touched it.

"Shall we?" Rupert held open the door for Josh.

Inside, the gallery was quiet and cool. They strolled around admiring the display of glass items and sculptures, all handblown by a local artist.

"These are gorgeous," Rupert said. "I think my mother might like something like this." He pointed to a glass sphere about the size of the palm of his hand. It was displayed in a place where it caught the light coming through the window and lit up the patterns of blue, turquoise, and white that rippled and swelled inside the clear glass. "It looks like waves, and she loves the ocean."

"It's beautiful," Josh agreed.

"And it's unique. I think it's perfect."

Decision made, Rupert went to talk to the person at the desk about purchasing it. Meanwhile Josh carried on looking at the other items on display. Lost in admiring a piece of stained glass that depicted a vase of flowers in shades of red, orange, and yellow, he didn't hear Rupert approach. He started at the warm hand on the small of his back.

"Sorry, didn't mean to make you jump." Rupert didn't take his hand away. Instead he slid it around Josh's waist as he stood close beside him. Josh leaned in a little and carried on staring at the colours where the light poured through.

"It's so pretty," Josh said.

"It's made your face multicoloured."

Josh turned and found Rupert staring at him rather than at the stained glass. Rupert had patches of bright colour on his skin from where the sun shone through the glass. "Yours too."

They smiled at each other, and their gazes locked and held. The warmth in Rupert's expression made Josh's breath catch.

Rupert was the one to break the spell. "Are you ready for lunch?"

"Yes." Josh moved to put a little distance between them. "Lunch sounds great."

## CHAPTER SEVEN

They managed to get a table by the window. Rupert gave the menu a cursory glance, but was distracted by Josh watching him read down the list of food. Josh's dark hair flopped over his forehead and he pushed it away. He looked tired, his face was paler than usual, and he had violet shadows under his eyes.

"What do you fancy?" Rupert asked.

Josh glanced up and gave him a small smile. "Um... I'm not sure."

"How about we get the platter of stuff to share?"

"Yeah, that sounds good."

"And to drink? Do you want beer? Oh no..." He flushed, cursing himself for not remembering. "Sorry. I forgot you don't drink."

"Lemonade for me. And no worries. I'm used to people thinking it's weird."

"It's not weird, and I should have remembered. Okay, I'll go and order."

He didn't have to wait long to order at the bar, and he returned a few minutes later with two bottles of still lemonade and glasses on a tray.

"Thanks," Josh said as Rupert passed one to him. "You could have had beer if you wanted it. I don't mind other people drinking."

"No, it's fine. I don't usually drink at lunchtime anyway."

Josh took a sip of his lemonade and then stirred it with his straw. The ice cubes clinked in the glass as he said, "I started drinking when I was thirteen and quit when I was seventeen. I haven't touched it since." He didn't meet Rupert's eyes.

"What changed?" Rupert asked.

"I drank so much vodka one night that I ended up in hospital having my stomach pumped. They told me I could have died. It was a wake-up call." His tone was light, but a muscle ticked in his jaw. He finally met Rupert's eyes. "It was the best thing that ever happened to me."

"Yeah?" Rupert prompted gently.

Josh had rarely told Rupert much about himself. He was opening up today in a way that was new, and Rupert wanted to do everything he could to encourage it.

"It got me to where I am now," Josh continued. "I realised I was turning into my dad, and I didn't want that for myself. So I stopped drinking—and doing any drugs I could find—and I went back to college."

"Good for you." Rupert was worried he sounded patronising, but he meant it. "It can't have been easy. I'm glad it worked out."

Josh gave him a small smile. "Thanks. Me too."

Their food arrived then, diverting them from the serious turn the conversation had taken.

The platter was a wonderful mixture of bread, olives, different cheeses, and dips. Lots of things that were delicious, but rather messy to eat. Once they'd tucked in and tried a few things, Josh asked, "So, when's your mother getting married?"

"In three weeks' time."

"Will it be a big wedding?"

"Oh, yes. My mother doesn't do anything by halves." Rupert tried to keep his voice light, but the bitterness seeped into his tone and Josh glanced up, brows raised.

"What's her fiancé like?"

Rupert couldn't hide his grimace. "He's… difficult. I can hardly have a civil conversation with him because he's so incredibly right-wing. He suits my mother, though."

"She's the same?"

Rupert nodded. "She's not quite as extreme as him, but yes. My political leanings are left of centre, like my dad's were. He was a socialist, stayed true to his working-class roots. He believed in sharing the wealth, prioritising education. He was the first person in his family to go to university, and that opportunity made all the difference to him. He always believed higher education should be funded by the state."

"God. I wish." Josh took another piece of bread. "Shame I wasn't born twenty years earlier. But I suppose having to work this hard for what I want means I'm taking it seriously. That's the only upside."

When they'd finished eating, Rupert ordered them coffees and they sat and chatted for a while longer. Josh seemed in no rush to leave. In Rupert's mind this was a date—albeit a date by stealth. He'd been thrilled when Josh had agreed to meet him for lunch, and was keen to prolong their time together as much as possible.

"Do you want to go for a walk or something?" Rupert asked when the waitress had cleared away their cups. "It's a gorgeous day today, and if you don't have to get back, I thought maybe we could walk along the harbour or get the ferry over to Mount Batten perhaps?"

Josh seemed to consider this for a minute, meeting Rupert's gaze while Rupert waited. Rupert could almost see the cogs whirring and wondered what thoughts were involved in the decision-making process.

"Okay," Josh said finally. "That'd be cool."

"You sure?" Rupert didn't want him to feel obliged. He wasn't paying Josh for today, after all… unless you counted buying lunch.

"Yeah. All I've done this week is work. I need a break today. I can get back to studying tomorrow."

"Great." Rupert smiled. "Let's go, then."

They ended up spending the whole afternoon together. They walked along the sea front and got the ferry across to Mount Batten peninsula. Josh insisted on paying the ferry fare. "No, it's okay. I've got this."

Later, he bought ice creams too. Rupert didn't argue. He sensed it was important to Josh to pay for what he saw as his share today, and he didn't want to make things awkward by protesting.

By the time they got the ferry back, it was getting close to dinner time. Rupert was pleasantly tired from walking and his nose felt warm where it had caught the sun. Josh's fair skin had more colour than earlier too. The heat of the day was gone, and the wind was chilly where it tugged at Rupert's shirt and whipped at his hair.

They stood at the stern, leaning against the railings, as the boat chugged through the water leaving a foamy white wake behind it. There were lots of small sailing boats out today and a few people in kayaks, all giving the ferry a wide berth to avoid the wash.

Rupert looked sidelong at Josh, noticing how the green of his eyes caught the sunlight. A few tiny freckles that Rupert hadn't noticed before speckled his nose. Maybe the sun today had brought them out. They stood close, their arms brushing where they held on to the rail, and Rupert was suddenly hit with a rush of longing. This afternoon had been wonderful, but he wasn't ready for the day to be over. He wanted more. He wanted Josh in his arms, and in his bed.

"Spend the evening with me," he blurted out. Josh turned, his brow furrowed, his mouth open to speak, but Rupert blundered on before he could think better of it. "I mean, I can pay you for it. Just like I normally do."

Josh's frown deepened. "I'm not sure. I should probably get back and do some more revision." He folded his arms tightly around himself and turned to look back at the water.

"But you said you needed a break today. Please?" Rupert cringed at the neediness in his tone, but his dignity was a small price to pay for more time with Josh. Rupert knew he wasn't behaving rationally. Josh was like a drug, making him desperate, craving for more.

Josh's expression was still tense, but the frown lifted a little. "It's short notice to book the hotel, but I could phone them, I suppose."

"You can come to mine... I mean, if you want. It would save you the cost of the room." He waited, tension rising as Josh bit his lip. Josh's tongue peeked out to worry at the silver ring.

"Okay," Josh finally said.

Rupert let out a shaky sigh of relief, a huge grin spreading across his face. "Cool."

A gust of wind sent one of Rupert's curls tumbling across his cheek, and he tucked it behind his ear. Josh smiled back at him, but he still looked uncertain. Rupert hoped Josh didn't think he was some creepy stalker. He didn't want to make Josh uncomfortable, but he wanted to be with him, any way he could.

Rupert unlocked the door to his flat and guided Josh in.

Josh whistled. "Nice place. Is this all yours?"

"Yeah." Rupert felt an uncomfortable mix of pride and guilt. His flat was the first place he'd owned, and he loved it. Thanks to his father's legacy, he didn't even have a mortgage. He was very aware that to Josh, owning a flat like this must make Rupert seem incredibly privileged. It wasn't too ostentatious — he could easily have afforded somewhere larger — but it was luxurious. On the top floor of a new build overlooking the harbour, it had two bedrooms and a large open-plan living area.

"It's so cool. One day I want to live somewhere like this." Josh's enthusiasm was obviously genuine, and Rupert relaxed a little. "Can I go outside?" Josh went over to the double doors that opened onto the roof garden.

"Of course." Rupert followed him out on the decking. It was only a small space but had a great view.

Josh turned and smiled at him, leaning back against the railings. "You're so lucky." Then his face fell. "I mean… to live here. But shit, I'm sorry. I know it's because of your dad, so that was really insensitive—"

Rupert moved a step closer. "It's okay." He put his hand on Josh's cheek. "I know what you meant." He kissed Josh's forehead. "Are you hungry?"

"Yes."

"Okay, let me go and see what I can rustle up."

"Want any help?"

"I'm not sure yet. Depends what I've got ingredients for."

Rupert got them both drinks first. Forgoing the bottle of red wine he'd normally have opened on a Saturday night, he had sparkling water with Josh. "Sorry I don't have any lime," he said as he passed the glass to Josh. "If I'd known you were coming, I'd have got some."

"No worries. Cheers." Josh raised his glass, and they clinked them together.

Rupert rummaged around in the fridge and found he had enough ingredients to throw together a stir-fry. He was out of noodles, but he had rice. He set Josh to work chopping onions, peppers, and mushrooms while he put the water on to heat for the rice and sliced a steak into thin strips.

The sight of Josh in his kitchen, helping him cook, made Rupert feel warm inside. It was so domestic, and it felt utterly right in a way that was equal parts exciting and terrifying.

*He's only here because I'm paying him*, Rupert reminded himself.

But Josh had met him for lunch earlier and spent the afternoon with him. Maybe eventually he could persuade Josh to date him for real? That didn't seem like such a complete impossibility after the day they'd just spent together.

They ate out on the roof garden, enjoying the last of the evening sunshine before the sun dropped out of sight. The warmth of the day had gone. Josh began to shiver in his thin T-shirt, so Rupert excused himself and returned with a hoodie, which he offered to Josh.

"Thanks." Josh took it gratefully and pulled it on, zipping it up and even pulling the hood up. He grinned at Rupert, his face shadowed by the fabric.

Rupert felt a fierce surge of possessiveness at the sight of Josh wearing something of his.

When they'd finished eating, Rupert insisted on clearing the plates. "It's okay, I can manage. Do you want a hot drink? Tea, coffee?"

"Coffee would be great. Might help me stay awake." Josh's tone was teasing. "I wouldn't want to fall asleep on you."

"Again."

Josh laughed. "I told you, it was a compliment. I don't fall asleep on just anyone, you know."

Rupert grinned. "Glad to hear it."

They sat side by side on the bench seat and watched the sun set as they drank their coffee. The sun painted the sky with streaks of pink and orange as it slowly inched its way below a smear of dark cloud on the horizon. Josh was still shivering despite the hoodie, so Rupert put his arm around him and pulled him close. Josh curled into his side, his hands wrapped around the mug and his face almost invisible because of the hood. It was a perfect moment, the ultimate romantic cliché. If this were a film or a novel, Rupert would be brave now and put words to all the things he didn't dare ask for. But the words went unspoken because Rupert was too afraid of what Josh's answer would be.

When the sun had finally gone and the sky was a deep blue fading fast to black, Josh climbed into Rupert's lap and kissed him. "Want to take this to the bedroom?" he asked.

Rupert didn't. Well, part of him did, of course. He always wanted Josh that way. But right then he was happy to be out there, cuddling and kissing and not taking any more than Josh wanted to give him. Josh's kisses were insistent, though, and his arousal seemed genuine. He tensed and shuddered as Rupert slid cold hands over the warm skin of his back, tugging him closer and grinding up against his arse.

"Yeah, okay," Rupert muttered between kisses. He licked over Josh's lip ring and into the plush heat of his mouth. Then he gripped Josh's thighs and grunted as he stood, thighs straining at the effort as he took Josh with him.

Josh clung to him like a monkey and chuckled into the kiss. "Impressive," he said. "You must do some good lifting at the gym."

Rupert carried him inside, and they carried on kissing as he made his way to the door of his bedroom.

"Ouch." Josh yelped. "Door handle."

Rupert's arms were aching now, but he managed to get Josh over to the bed before he dropped him. Josh bounced on the mattress, legs akimbo, and laughing as he rubbed his hip. "That's gonna bruise."

"Sorry." Rupert grinned. "These things are always so much more romantic in the movies than in real life."

"Romantic?" Josh raised his eyebrows.

Rupert's cheeks heated. It was a stupid word to have used in this context. "Whatever." He lowered himself over Josh and kissed him as a distraction.

It worked. There wasn't much talking for a while as they got swept up in the heat of the moment. Rupert took his time, undressing Josh and himself between deep, searing kisses that stole his breath.

Finally they were naked, lying on their sides facing each other. Josh circled Rupert's cock with his hand and tugged gently, teasingly, making Rupert moan with frustration. "What do you want this evening?" Josh asked. "My hand, my mouth, my arse?"

Rupert suddenly realised they hadn't discussed how many hours Josh would stay, and also — with a flash of shame — that he hadn't paid Josh in advance tonight as he usually would. Maybe Josh hadn't wanted to ask him for it? But now didn't feel like the right time to bring it up, not when they were both naked and horny. Josh obviously trusted Rupert to pay him later.

Josh's lips were already wet from their kisses, and he licked them again as he waited for Rupert's answer. The teasing sweep of his tongue helped Rupert decide. "Your mouth," he said huskily. "I want your mouth on me." He was about to roll over to get a condom from the drawer by the bed, but Josh was already wriggling down. He sucked Rupert into the slick heat of his mouth before Rupert could protest.

"Fuck," he groaned, sliding his fingers into Josh's silky dark hair. "Oh God, that feels good… but don't you want a condom?"

Josh shook his head, still sucking. He hummed, pulling off for a moment to meet Rupert's eyes and say. "Do I need one?"

Rupert shook his head.

"Well, then. I want to do it like this." He parted his lips and took Rupert back inside, his gaze still fixed on Rupert, watching as Rupert cursed, his fingers tightening in Josh's hair.

He took Rupert deep in long, slow strokes. The head of Rupert's cock bumped the back of his throat each time. Josh stroked Rupert's balls with his other hand, his careful fingers squeezing and tugging, then reaching back farther to stroke Rupert's perineum. Instinctively, Rupert lifted his leg, putting it on Josh's shoulder to allow him access.

Josh looked up at him again, eyebrows raised as if in question as he hummed around Rupert's cock.

"Fuck, *yes*." Rupert's voice was high and embarrassingly close to a whimper as Josh circled his hole with a dry fingertip. It burned as Josh slipped it in, just a little, but Rupert opened for him anyway, pushing greedily against the intrusion.

Josh pulled off again to ask, "Lube?"

"I'll get it." Rupert rolled onto his back to reach into the drawer. "Here."

Josh moved between Rupert's thighs now and pushed his knees until they were bent, feet flat on the bed. He took the bottle and teased Rupert for a moment, pressing kisses to his thighs and taint, licking his balls, until Rupert made a strangled sound of protest.

"Please, Josh."

And then Josh's fingers were back, slick with lube now. As he slid one into Rupert, he sucked on Rupert's cock again. The dual sensation made Rupert cry out, clutching at the sheets as Josh added another finger. The stretch was almost too much, but he wanted it. It had been a while since he'd fingered himself, longer still since he'd been fucked. He imagined how Josh's cock would feel inside him, how Josh would look fucking him, and suddenly he knew that was what he wanted tonight. Not Josh's hand, not his mouth, not his arse. He wanted his cock. But with Josh's fingers moving inside him and that gorgeous mouth sucking on him so perfectly, he was close already.

"Stop," he managed.

Josh froze. With his fingers still inside Rupert, he let Rupert's cock slip from his mouth. "Sorry. Is this too much? I thought you wanted—"

"No. I do." He swallowed. But… I want you to fuck me."

Surprise registered on Josh's face, but then his lips curved into a smile so sweet and sexy it made Rupert's cock jerk. "Yeah?"

"Only if you want?" Rupert said. "You don't have to." He didn't want Josh to feel he had to do anything just because Rupert was paying him. He wanted Josh to *want* it, like he did.

"Oh yeah. I definitely want to fuck you. Now?"

"Yes." Rupert wasn't sure he was prepped enough, but he couldn't wait. He needed Josh inside him.

"Okay."

While Josh rolled a condom on and made himself slick, Rupert reached down and tentatively thrust two fingers into himself, spreading them and working himself open a little more.

"Fuck, you look good like that," Josh said.

Rupert snapped his gaze up to Josh's face. Josh was watching him intently, toying with the ring in his lip with his tongue. Rupert's cock flexed with a pulse of arousal from Josh's words, leaking precome into the hair on his belly. He spread his legs a little wider and pushed his fingers deeper, giving Josh a show.

Josh smoothed his hands down the strong muscles of Rupert's thighs. "You ready for me?"

"Uh-huh." Rupert withdrew his fingers and let Josh move in to take their place. He bit back a moan as Josh deliberately slid the tip of his cock slowly back and forth over Rupert's hole. "Come *on*, Josh."

Josh gave it to him, pushing in smoothly and lowering his body to cover Rupert's as he did so. Rupert moaned and arched up to meet him, pulling Josh down for a messy, desperate kiss as their bodies moved together and found a rhythm. Josh rocked into him slowly and carefully. Rupert was grateful for his patience, because it hurt at first. The pain was right on the edge of what he could stand, but he didn't want to ask Josh to stop. He parted his lips, deepening the kiss and moaning as Josh rolled his hips, pushing in a little deeper. Gradually the pain morphed into bone-deep pleasure, spiralling out from his centre and lighting up his whole body. Everything was warm skin, sensation, and perfect pressure inside him as Josh fucked him harder and faster. Josh broke the kiss to sit back a little. He pushed Rupert's knees up, changing the angle to make it even better. Josh's cheeks had flushed pink, and he bit his lip, brow furrowed with concentration. He was so beautiful.

"Fuck," Rupert grunted as Josh rubbed his prostate just right, every thrust sending sparks of sensation through him.

"You gonna come soon?" Josh panted. Sweat gleamed on his skin.

"Think so." Rupert reached down to jerk himself off.

"Thank *fuck*."

Rupert huffed out a breathless laugh that turned into a groan at the tight slide of his hand. "God, yeah…." Just a few more strokes were all he needed before he came, his body locking tight at the blinding pleasure of it. He was dimly aware of Josh gasping out his name, his rhythm faltering as he fucked in hard one last time and stilled, shuddering over Rupert as he came too.

Josh's arms gave out and he flopped forwards, his face buried in Rupert's neck as their ragged breathing settled.

Rupert put his arms around Josh and held him tight—maybe too tight, but he couldn't bring himself to loosen his grip. He didn't trust himself to speak in case something stupid came out. This was too much. His feelings were overwhelming, and he was terrified of giving himself away.

Eventually Josh made a muffled sound of protest and pushed up, so Rupert had to let him go, but Josh didn't move far. He just rolled onto his back beside Rupert to pull off the condom.

"Bin?" He sounded exhausted.

Rupert plucked the condom from his fingers. "I'll deal with it."

When he came back from the bathroom, Josh was curled on his side, eyes closed and breathing deeply. Rupert slipped into the bed behind him and pressed a cautious kiss to the star tattoo at the top of his spine.

"Josh?" he whispered.

No response.

Rupert wondered whether he should wake him. But Josh had been studying hard all week. He needed sleep. This way he'd get more rest than if Rupert sent him home, plus having Josh in his bed all night was more than Rupert could resist. So he turned out the light and curled his body carefully around Josh, bare skin against bare skin. Josh stirred when Rupert put a hand lightly on his hip, but only to snuggle closer, and then he was still again.

## CHAPTER EIGHT

Josh drifted slowly into consciousness. Warm and comfortable with the scent of something—or someone—familiar surrounding him, he came to realise he was still in Rupert's bed. He lay unmoving, cataloguing the sounds of the seagulls outside, the morning sunshine filtering in around the edges of the blinds, and the soft huff of Rupert's breath where he lay sprawled on his back beside Josh. Josh had his arm thrown over Rupert's chest, and it moved gently with each rise and fall of Rupert's ribs. He shifted his hand a fraction and felt the tickle of hair against his palm.

Josh lifted his head from where it had somehow nestled into Rupert's armpit in the night and squinted at Rupert's face in the half-light. He looked serene. Deeply asleep with his lips slightly parted, Rupert didn't even stir as Josh shifted up onto his elbow. Josh leaned over and pressed a kiss to Rupert's cheek; soft stubble tickled his lips as he breathed in Rupert's scent. Josh smiled, a warm rush of affection flooding him. He knew it was dangerous to let himself feel it, but he couldn't tamp it down. He'd crossed so many lines with Rupert already, but he was past caring. Like an out-of-control car with the brake cable cut, he was hurtling headlong into unknown territory, and all he could do was hang on and ride it out, hoping the damage at the end wouldn't be too disastrous.

*Fuck it.*

Josh slid down the bed, taking the covers part of the way with him. He leaned over Rupert's groin and kissed his cock where it lay soft, but plump. His mouth watered in anticipation, and he kissed it again, using his tongue on the soft skin until it began to firm up. Josh guided Rupert's cock into his mouth, sucking as it hardened and thickened. Rupert finally stirred and muttered, "Josh?"

"Mm-hmm," Josh replied, his mouth too full for words.

Rupert grunted and slid a hand into Josh's hair, stroking his scalp lightly. "'S good."

Josh carried on sucking, tasting sweet saltiness as Rupert got harder still. Focused on making Rupert feel good, he was only dimly aware of his own erection at first. But Josh's arousal became more pressing as Rupert's breathing thickened and another burst of salty precome bloomed on his tongue. He reached down to stroke himself, not trying to come but easing the ache, gripping and sliding his hand lazily as he sucked.

"I'm getting close," Rupert warned him.

Josh considered pulling off, and maybe it was reckless and stupid, but he wanted to feel Rupert come in his mouth. He wanted Rupert inside him in every way he could have him. He trusted Rupert. He didn't know what Rupert thought about it, but he wasn't just a client to Josh, not anymore. He took Rupert deep, sucking hard and greedily until Rupert climaxed with a hoarse groan, hips flexing up as he filled Josh's mouth with his come. Josh carried on sucking for a little longer, more gently, and then finally pulled away to swallow. He licked his lips and grinned at Rupert, who guided him up the bed for a kiss.

Josh's dick poked Rupert in the leg, and he took the hint, wrapping his hand around it and stroking. Josh straddled him, fucking into the grip of Rupert's hand as he kissed him. It was a sloppy, open-mouthed kiss and Josh knew Rupert would be able to taste the last traces of his release that still lingered. Josh came without breaking the kiss. Rupert's tongue in his mouth stifled his moan of pleasure as he spilled over Rupert's fist, making a mess between them.

Slowly the kiss turned gentler, less desperate, the hunger replaced by sweet affection and teasing nips and brushes of lips. At last, Josh pushed up on his hands and looked down at Rupert, who smiled back, lazy and sated. Rupert's red curls were a wild tangle on the white pillowcase. The soft expression on his face made Josh's heart flip hopefully.

"Good morning," Josh said, his voice rough from sleep and deep-throating.

"Morning." Rupert brought a hand up and pushed Josh's hair out of his eyes. "That was a fun way to wake up."

"I aim to please," Josh said lightly.

The light in Rupert's expression went out as though a switch had been flipped. Josh's own smile faded as he realised he'd somehow said the wrong thing. He was about to try and smooth it over, but Rupert spoke first.

"Are you hungry?" He patted Josh's hip, encouraging him to move so he could slide out from underneath him. Rupert turned away, his back to Josh as he picked up his discarded shirt from the day before and wiped Josh's come off his hand and stomach.

"I guess."

"Go and clean up. I'll get the kettle on and see what food I've got. Do you want tea or coffee?" There was a cold formality to his tone that made anxiety churn in Josh's stomach. He stared at the broad expanse of Rupert's back, tension in every line of muscle. The intimacy from before was all gone. What had he done wrong?

"Coffee, please," Josh said unhappily, wishing he could turn the clock back five minutes and start this conversation over.

Josh picked up his clothes and took them to the bathroom. When he emerged, he went to find Rupert in the kitchen.

"Coffee's in the pot," Rupert said. "There's milk in the fridge and sugar by the kettle." He still sounded brusque, but was more cheerful again. He avoided Josh's eyes, though, busying himself with pulling ingredients out of the fridge and assembling them on the worktop. "Is an omelette okay with you? I've got ham and cheese I can put in it, and some mushrooms, I think." He rummaged at the back of the fridge again. "Yes, mushrooms too."

"Sounds great, thanks. Need any help?"

"No, I can manage."

Josh poured his coffee and sat on a stool at the breakfast bar that divided the kitchen from the living area. Rupert was efficient, chopping and frying, whisking and grating. Josh was impressed at his level of activity, considering it was still pretty early on a Sunday morning. He wasn't a morning person, and he was still unsettled by the slightly frosty atmosphere between them. His brain wasn't awake enough to attempt small talk, so he watched in silence, enjoying the way Rupert's arse jiggled in his sweatpants as he whisked the eggs.

They ate out on the balcony. It was a beautiful morning, still cool, but full of the promise of summer heat later in the day.

"I wish I didn't have exams to revise for," Josh said. "It's going to be a perfect day, and I'll be stuck indoors studying again."

"How many more exams have you got?"

"Only three. Monday, Thursday, and then my last one on Friday morning. I can't wait. I need a break from the books."

"What are your plans for the summer?" Rupert asked.

"Nothing much. I'm staying in Plymouth, working as usual. My housemates will be around some of the time, so I'll have company."

"You're not going on holiday at all?"

"No." Josh had considered it. Dani had tried to persuade him to go for a week in Ibiza with her boyfriend and some of their mates. But Josh didn't want to blow a few hundred quid on it. He didn't mind chaperoning drunken people around sometimes, but for that many nights in a row, it would get old fast. "What about you? You going away?"

Rupert shook his head. "No. I suppose if I get the urge, I might book something at short notice, or maybe go and visit some friends."

When they'd finished eating, Rupert offered Josh more coffee, but he declined.

"No, I'm going to have to make a move soon. Get home and start on my revision. But thanks for breakfast. It was great." He stood and picked up his plate, then reached for Rupert's too. "Let me help clear up before I go, though."

Rupert followed him to the kitchen and stacked things in the dishwasher while Josh washed the omelette pan. Washing up done, Josh gathered his things and sat on the sofa to put on his shoes.

"How much do I owe you?" Rupert asked.

Josh snapped his head up to meet Rupert's gaze. His heart lurched. He'd forgotten Rupert was supposed to pay him. Rupert stood in front of him with his wallet in his hand.

"Um... I don't know. Just call it an hour, for last night?" Josh barely managed to make the words sound normal around the uncomfortable lump growing in his throat.

"But you've been here all night."

The lump turned bitter, acid spreading through Josh's veins.

"For fuck's sake, Rupert. I'm not charging you for sleeping next to me." His voice came out sharp, betraying his hurt and anger. He took a deep breath to steady himself. This wasn't Rupert's fault. Josh had never told Rupert this was anything other than a normal client relationship for him. He only had himself to blame for things getting awkward now. He should never have agreed to spend time with Rupert that wasn't on the clock. "An hour for last night is fine."

"But you.... We did stuff again this morning." Rupert frowned, his face flushed. "I don't want to take advantage of you."

"You're not. Look... I sucked your cock this morning because I wanted to, okay? Think of it as a freebie. Pro boner, if you will." Josh forced a grin, trying to sound convincingly amused by his own joke, but probably failing if the unhappy expression on Rupert's face was anything to go by.

"Newsflash: I've occasionally been known to have sex with people for reasons other than cold, hard cash." He stood, ready to leave. He wanted out of this situation before he gave himself away.

"Okay. I'm sorry."

"Don't worry about it."

Rupert opened his wallet and counted out some notes. "This is for last night, then." He stepped forward, offering them to Josh.

Josh stared at the money for a moment, hesitating. He didn't want it, but it was easier to take it than to explain.

"Thanks." He took the cash and shoved it into his pocket. "And thanks for dinner and breakfast too."

"You're welcome."

They stood facing each other, just a short distance apart, but it felt like a million miles. Josh remembered the easy intimacy of last night, the happiness he'd felt on waking up this morning, and wondered where the fuck it had all gone wrong. Maybe the closeness was all an illusion and Josh only saw it because he wanted to believe it was there. With Rupert's money burning a hole in his pocket, he felt more like a whore than he ever had in nearly two years of selling his body.

"Okay, I'd better go. Bye, Rupert."

Josh turned before Rupert could reach for him. If Rupert touched him, he was afraid he'd shatter like glass and fall apart into fractured pieces.

Rupert saw him to the door, but he must have sensed the mood because he made no move to hug or kiss Josh goodbye.

"Good luck with the rest of your exams." He added, "I'll call you," as Josh walked down the corridor to the lift.

Josh didn't answer, and as the lift doors slid open, he heard Rupert's door bang shut.

Josh felt sick as he walked home. The blue sky and sunshine did nothing to lift his spirits. All they did was highlight his own black mood. Back at the house he bypassed the sound of voices in the living room and went straight up the stairs, heading for his room on the top floor.

On the first floor landing, he nearly ran into Jez, coming out of the bathroom dressed in a pair of boxers. He had love bites all over his chest and wore the slightly dazed expression and flushed cheeks of someone who'd recently come.

He grinned at Josh. "Hi, mate. Good night?"

"Not bad," Josh replied, ducking away from Jez's gaze and trying to get past him. He wasn't in the mood for conversation.

Jez frowned. "Are you okay?"

"Yeah, just tired."

Jez didn't look convinced.

"Jez! Hurry up and come back to bed," Mac called from Jez's room.

Jez put his hand on Josh's arm. "Are you sure you're all right?"

"I'm fine. But your boyfriend needs you. Don't keep him waiting." Josh managed a grin as he squeezed past Jez, but his heart twisted with envy for what Jez and Mac had together. It must be nice to have a boyfriend to snuggle with on a Sunday morning.

In his room Josh spread out his books and revision notes and tried to focus, but his mind kept wandering. When he found himself staring out of the window for the umpteenth time, he sighed heavily and forced himself to look back at the words on the page. He read them, but they could have been Greek for all the sense they made to him today. He needed to concentrate. The exams this year went towards his final degree. He was *not* going to fuck them up because of Rupert. He got a notepad and a pen and started writing things down, forcing his brain to process the words by rewriting his revision notes.

A gentle knock on the door pulled him back to reality. He looked at the time on his phone and realised a couple of hours had passed.

"Come in," he called.

"Hi." Dani came into the room with two steaming mugs. "I was making coffee, so I brought you some."

"Oh, thanks." Josh took mug she held out to him. "You're a star. I'm ready for a caffeine boost." Dani sat on his bed, and Josh turned his chair around to face her. "How's revision going?"

"Slowly," she said. "But I'm getting there." There was silence for a moment, and then Dani asked, "Are you okay, Josh?"

"Yeah. Why?" The response was instinctive, if not entirely honest.

"Well. You were supposed to only be meeting Rupert for lunch, but ended up staying out all night. And then Jez told me you looked pissed off when you came back this morning. So what's up?" Her tone implied that she wasn't going to let him fob her off with a vague answer.

Josh put his mug down and rubbed his face with his hands. "Ugh," he said eloquently. When he met Dani's gaze again, she was looking at him expectantly.

"I don't know. I'm confused about this thing with Rupert. One minute he's treating me like a friend — more than a friend, even — and then the next minute he's giving me money to fuck him again. Yesterday was great. We had lunch and hung out together all afternoon, but then he asked me to go home with him and offered to pay me. Maybe I should have said no...."

"But you didn't?"

"I said yes. He is a client, after all, so what else was I going to do? Plus I *wanted* to go home with him." As soon as he said the words, he knew he'd got to the crux of it. "I wanted to go home with him, and I would have gone even if he hadn't offered me money." The lump in his throat was back and his eyes stung. "Then we had an amazing night together, I slept in his bed, woke up with him beside me... and then this morning we had this epically awkward conversation about how much money he owed me. We haggled over whether he should pay me for morning sex or not. Jesus Christ. It's so fucked up."

"Oh, honey. Get over here." Dani put her coffee down and held out her arms.

The sympathy on Dani's face made the floodgates open. Hot, frustrated tears spilled out of Josh's eyes as he stumbled across the room and into her tight embrace. She hugged him, stroking his hair and making soothing noises while he got himself back under control enough to talk.

"It made me feel like shit. I don't want his money anymore."

"But what do you think he wants? It sounds as if he likes you too. None of your other clients take you out for lunch or have you sleep in their beds all night. You've been meeting him for drinks before every appointment. He's been paying you for more than just sex. He's basically been paying you to be his boyfriend for a while now."

Josh pulled back, sniffing and wiping his nose on his sleeve. "Do you reckon?"

He hadn't thought about it like that. He knew Rupert liked him, it was obvious. But he still thought it was mostly about sex, maybe a little companionship too, but that wasn't unusual with clients. It didn't mean Rupert wanted him as anything other than an escort.

"It sounds that way to me. But maybe he thinks he can only have you if he keeps paying."

"But even if he does like me, I can't be his boyfriend."

"Why not?"

"Why do you think?" Josh snapped, frustrated. "What boyfriend is going to put up with my job? I know Rupert doesn't like it when I see other clients. It's obvious. So he'd never handle it if we were in a relationship. Plus how on earth could we transition from him paying me for sex to actually being a couple? I don't see how it could ever work when we've started out like this. It's a business relationship, and it needs to stay that way."

She shrugged. "Seems like you've been doing a pretty good job of crossing that line already. If you both want the same thing, then I'm sure you could make it work. But not unless you're honest with each other about what you really want."

"What on earth would I say to him? 'Oh, hey. This is awkward, but I have feelings for you, so how about you stop paying me for sex and we date instead?' Yeah. I don't think so, Dani. I already feel stupid for falling for him. I can't tell him how I feel."

"You could," she said. "You could just say the words and see what happens."

Josh shook his head. "No way." He didn't see how Rupert could ever be anything other than a client, and he blamed himself for letting Rupert get too close.

"Well"—she patted his leg—"you don't have to rush into anything. You won't be seeing him again till next weekend, will you? So you've got some time to think about it."

"Yeah."

Josh was sure he wouldn't think about much else all week.

## CHAPTER NINE

Rupert stripped the bed after Josh left. The sheets were messed up from the night before, and it gave him something to do as he went over the awkward conversation they'd had that morning.

Rupert was confused by Josh's reaction. Surely Josh had expected Rupert to pay him? They weren't dating, as much as Rupert wished they were. But this morning Josh had looked as though he didn't want Rupert's money. He'd seemed… hurt, offended almost. Rupert sighed as he shoved the sheets viciously into the washing machine and slammed the door.

He'd never meant things to get so complicated. Maybe he should be honest with Josh about his feelings. But he'd asked Josh on a date before, and Josh had declined. Rupert didn't think the answer would be any different if he tried again. So he had two choices: cut contact with Josh, or carry on paying him and take what he could get.

He knew which of those was the sensible option, but he also knew it wasn't going to happen. He couldn't let Josh go.

He texted Josh on Monday to wish him luck with his exam. He didn't get a reply until the afternoon, and when it came it was just one word: *Thanks*.
*How did it go?*
*Not bad.*

Rupert didn't know what to say after that, and he wasn't getting a chatty vibe from Josh, so he left it.

He didn't hear anything from Josh all week, but knew he was busy with revision. Rupert waited till Friday afternoon to call, remembering Josh's last exam was that morning.

Josh picked up after a few rings. "Hey, Rupert."

Rupert could hear lots of other voices in the background. "Hi." He leaned back in his seat and tried to suppress the goofy smile that stretched across his face, simply from hearing Josh's voice. "How were the exams this week?"

"I think they went okay." Raucous laughter burst out in the background. "Hang on, it's too noisy in here. I'm gonna move."

Rupert listened to the muffled sound of movement for a few moments, and then Josh was back. "That's better. I'm outside now. I was in the pub with people from my course."

"Are you free later?" Rupert asked. "If you are, I'd like to see you."

"Um... no. Sorry."

Josh didn't give an explanation. Rupert hoped it was because he was going to stay out with his friends, but he knew Josh usually saw clients on a Friday.

"How about tomorrow, then?"

There was a short pause. "Do you mean for an appointment?" Josh's voice was cautious.

"Um." Rupert felt put on the spot, and wondered what the right answer was. "Well... yeah."

It was silent on the other end of the phone for long enough that Rupert thought he'd been cut off. But then Josh finally spoke.

"No. Sorry… I don't think I'm free. I think I booked someone else in."

If Rupert had been in any doubt that he was way too involved, the hot rush of jealousy that flooded through him would have clued him in.

"Oh, right. No worries." He got the words out through gritted teeth.

"I have an assignment to finish before the end of term, so I'm pretty busy next week, but I might be able to see you at the weekend. I'll let you know."

"Okay, thanks."

"I've got to go. Bye, Rupert."

"Bye."

The line went dead.


Rupert managed to stop himself from calling Josh again. The weekend crawled by, and the next week didn't go any faster. He found himself wondering how Josh had done in his exams, and hoped his hard work had paid off.

When he hadn't heard from Josh by Friday, Rupert was starting to go a little crazy. It had been almost two weeks since he'd seen Josh, and he was shocked by how much he missed him.

He finally cracked and texted Josh in the morning. Just asking, *Can I see you tonight?* But Josh still hadn't replied by lunchtime, and Rupert started to think Josh was avoiding him.

"Surely you should be looking happier at the prospect of some time off?" Georgina asked.

They'd met for lunch in the cafe at the Student Union and were now drinking coffee and sharing a huge piece of chocolate cake.

Rupert had a couple of weeks of holiday coming up, but he hadn't made any plans and wasn't particularly excited about it.

"I don't have any plans, though, so I'll just be kicking around at home with nothing to do." Rupert put his fork down. He wasn't hungry. He'd only agreed to share the cake with Georgina because it was so obvious she wanted it, but wouldn't have ordered it unless he'd agreed.

"Yeah, yeah. Such a hard life, all that free time." She grinned before popping in another mouthful and chewing with gusto.

Rupert let his gaze drift over her shoulder, and he stiffened when he caught sight of a guy in the queue for coffee. The slim build and dark hair were familiar, and there was something about his posture too… but it wasn't the first time he'd caught sight of someone around the university who looked a little like Josh. He tried to focus on what Georgina was saying to him, but then the man in the queue turned, and Rupert caught sight of his profile.

It was definitely, unmistakably Josh.

"Rupert!" Georgina's voice made Rupert jump and blush.

"Sorry, I was distracted." He couldn't stop his gaze from flicking back to Josh again.

"I noticed." She glanced over her shoulder just as Josh caught sight of Rupert and gave an awkward wave and a small smile that made Rupert's stomach flip with hope.

"Ohhh," she said knowingly, drawing out the word. "Josh, I presume?"

Rupert nodded, turning back to Georgina, who was looking at him with the expression of a cat focusing its attention on some small, unsuspecting rodent.

"He's cute. You're still seeing him, then?"

"Sort of."

"What does that mean?"

Rupert squirmed, not liking the turn this conversation was taking. "I don't know. It's just casual." He glanced over at Josh again, who was paying for his coffee.

After taking his change and the cup, Josh had to pass right by their table. He kept his head down, avoiding Rupert's gaze, and for a moment Rupert thought he was going to walk right past without acknowledging him again. But as Josh got closer, he looked up.

"Hi," he said, but made as if to carry on past without stopping.

"Hi, how are you?" Rupert asked quickly. "Do you want to join us if you've got a minute?" He gestured to a free chair at their table.

"Um... yeah, okay. Thanks." Josh pulled out the chair and sat.

"This is Georgina. Georgina, this is Josh."

"Nice to meet you, Josh." She offered her hand with a grin and Josh took it to shake. "Rupert's told me about you."

Josh glanced sidelong at Rupert, and Rupert's cheeks heated. "Good things, I hope?"

"He didn't go into details," Georgina replied.

"So, did you get your results yet?" Rupert asked. He wanted to get the subject away from their relationship — such as it was — as soon as possible.

"Yeah." Josh smiled widely for the first time. "I got them this morning. I got a first."

"That's fantastic. Well done." Rupert wanted to reach out and take his hand, or pull him into a hug. But with Georgina there, he was self-conscious.

Georgina echoed Rupert's congratulations, then started quizzing Josh about his course. Josh answered her questions, and Rupert listened, watching Josh's hands as he curled them around his cup and the curve of his lips as he smiled at something Georgina said.

After a few minutes, Georgina made a show of looking at the time on her phone and excusing herself. "I'm so sorry, but I have to dash. I have a meeting starting in five minutes. But it was really nice to meet you, Josh."

Rupert tried not to show his disbelief. She hadn't mentioned any meeting to him when they'd agreed to have lunch together, and normally she'd have stayed and chatted for longer. He stood to give her a hug and a kiss on the cheek.

"See you soon, Rupert," she said. "Hope to meet you again, Josh. Bye."

And then she was gone, leaving them alone together.

Rupert picked up his cup and then realised it was empty. When he raised his eyes to Josh, Josh was picking at a scratch on the table with his fingernail.

"That's great news about your exams," Rupert finally said.

Josh looked up and grinned. "Yeah. I'm dead chuffed."

"You deserve it. You work bloody hard. Well…. It sounds as if you do."

Josh dipped his finger into the foam on his coffee and transferred some to his mouth. He licked his finger clean, and Rupert watched, distracted by Josh's lips and tongue. When Josh raised his eyes and caught Rupert watching him, Rupert flushed and looked away quickly, picking up a napkin and wiping at a drop of coffee on the table for something to do.

"Um… did you get my text earlier?" Rupert asked, hating how needy he sounded, but persevering anyway. "I was wondering if you were free tonight?"

"Oh, sorry. No. The sound on my phone was off for a meeting with my tutor, and I forgot to turn it back on."

"So, are you? Free, I mean?"

Josh hesitated and Rupert's heart beat fast, he realised he'd clenched his fist tight around the napkin while he waited for Josh's reply.

"Yes," Josh said eventually. "I can see you tonight."

Rupert relaxed a little, but he was still wary. Josh's expression was closed and didn't give much away. Rupert knew he'd messed up the other weekend at his flat and something had changed, but he wasn't sure how to fix it—or whether it was possible.

"Do you want to come to mine again?" he asked.

"No. I'll book a room." Josh's tone was firm. He met Rupert's gaze, and there was… not coldness, exactly, but a distance that Rupert hated. "I think that's best."

Rupert swallowed against a swell of disappointment. "Okay." Seeing Josh in a hotel room was better than not seeing him at all. But he'd rather have Josh in his bed. "Is eight o'clock okay? Can you meet for a drink first?"

"Not tonight, sorry. I'll meet you at the hotel. Do you want one hour, or more?"

Rupert's heart deflated. It was obvious Josh was trying to get things back to a more businesslike footing between them. He could tell when he was being given the brush-off. "One's fine," he muttered and then stood, needing some space. "Okay, I'd better get back to work. I'll see you later."

"Bye," Josh said.

"Bye." Rupert walked away without looking back.

Later in the afternoon, Georgina called while Rupert was finishing up some paperwork in his poky cubicle that served as an office. He didn't pick up the first time because he wasn't in the mood to chat. But when his phone rang again immediately and he saw it was her again, he gave in and answered it.

"Hi," he said flatly. "What's up?"

"You sound cheerful. I thought you'd be happier after seeing Josh. He's adorable by the way; I can see why you like him. How did it go?"

"Fine." He had no wish to discuss Josh with her. "Anyway, sorry, Georgina, but I can't talk for long now. Did you want something?"

"Yes. I'm really sorry to do this at such short notice, but I'm afraid I can't make the wedding next weekend, after all. Something's come up."

"What exactly?" Rupert asked, immediately suspicious.

"It's a conference in Germany. One of my senior colleagues was supposed to be going, but she's broken her leg and they've asked me to go in her place."

Rupert sighed. "Okay. I suppose it can't be helped."

"But you should ask Josh. I bet he'd love to go with you, and it would be a good opportunity to spend more time with him. Two nights away in a hotel, a whole day in between, travelling together—"

"Georgina. This had better be a real conference."

"Of course it's real. Don't be ridiculous. Anyway, I've got to go. Sorry again to leave you in the lurch. Have a good weekend, and I'll see you soon."

"Okay. Bye."

"Bye." Her voice was suspiciously breezy, and then the line went dead.

Rupert put his phone aside and rested his chin on his hand as he stared out of his office window and weighed up his options. He could tell his mother he'd be coming alone and put up with her grumbling about messing up the numbers at the last minute. No doubt there would be some complicated table plan that hinged on having exactly the expected number of people. Or...

He could find someone else to go with him.

He ran through a mental list of female friends and acquaintances, but most of them were busy people with partners or families. No way would any of them be able to give up a whole weekend at such short notice to accompany him to a wedding.

Inevitably his thoughts turned to one person he'd actually like to spend a weekend with.

*Josh.*

He remembered his mother's email and the conversation he'd had with her a few weeks back, and his hackles rose. How dare she expect him to play straight for her wedding just to keep Charles happy?

Rupert should never have invited Georgina in the first place. Fake conference or not, she was doing him a favour by cancelling. Rupert would rather take a man as his plus-one and have the satisfaction of being true to himself, even if he had to pay Josh to do it.

He'd ask him tonight. Josh seemed determined to keep things strictly business between them, so Rupert would play that game. Josh was an escort, after all, and Rupert didn't care how much it would cost to book him for the whole weekend. If Josh would do it, Rupert would pay him any amount of money. He'd make Josh an offer he couldn't afford to refuse.

## CHAPTER TEN

Rupert was deliberately ten minutes late for their appointment that evening. He didn't want to seem too desperate—even though he was. Josh was lodged under his skin like a splinter, worming his way closer to Rupert's heart with every meeting.

Josh had texted him the room number, and when Rupert knocked on the door, Josh called, "It's open."

Rupert entered to find Josh sitting on the edge of the bed. He was barefoot, but still wearing jeans and a T-shirt. His smile didn't reach his eyes and he didn't stand to greet Rupert like he normally did.

"Hi, how are you?" Josh asked.

"Not bad."

Rupert locked the door and went to stand between Josh's knees. He wanted to pull Josh up and kiss him, to coax a reaction out of him that was more than sexual. But Josh's expression was shuttered, and Rupert had no idea what was going on behind those cool green eyes.

Josh looked up at him, licked his lips, and swallowed. "What do you want tonight?"

"I want to fuck you." Rupert's voice came out more roughly than he'd intended.

"Okay." Josh stood, still meeting Rupert's gaze. "Have you got the money?"

Rupert felt the words like a punch in the gut. A stark reminder of exactly what this was and how stupid he'd been to imagine it could ever be more.

He pulled his wallet out of his back pocket and counted out the notes. Then he handed them to Josh, who shoved them into his pocket.

"Thanks." Josh lifted his T-shirt over his head then and tossed it aside. The birds tattooed on his chest were stark against his pale skin in the dim light of the room. He made no move to kiss Rupert, and Rupert didn't reach for him either.

"Get the rest of your clothes off." Rupert unbuckled and unzipped, just pushing his trousers and underwear down enough to get his cock out. He wasn't hard yet, so he stroked himself roughly a few times until he began to stiffen.

"Want some help with that? I can suck you?" Josh offered.

Rupert shook his head, cheeks heating with a flush that was more anger than embarrassment. "No. Get on the bed.... Not like that, on your hands and knees." He didn't want to see Josh's face tonight, and he was afraid his own expression might betray him. He wanted too much—so much more than Josh was prepared to give him.

Josh knelt, legs spread. He was hard even though Rupert hadn't touched him yet. If nothing else, he obviously wanted Rupert physically. Rupert picked up the lube and a condom from the bedside table and moved in behind Josh. His hole was tight and dry. He hadn't prepped himself for tonight at least, but that was the only sign he was treating Rupert differently to any other client.

"Get yourself ready." Rupert tossed the lube down on the bed, and then watched as Josh slicked his fingers and worked two into his arse. The sight of that got Rupert all the way hard, and he stroked his cock slowly while Josh opened himself up.

"I'm good to go," Josh said.

"Don't stop. You look hot like that." Rupert tore open the wrapper and rolled the condom down his length mostly by feel. His gaze was still fixed on Josh's fingers, where he was sliding them in and out of his tight pink hole.

"Okay." Rupert moved in close, gripping his cock at the base as Josh pulled his fingers out.

Rupert thrust inside with one hard push of his hips. Josh gasped, a small shocked sound, and Rupert stilled then. "All right?"

"Yeah. Fine. You surprised me, that's all."

Rupert put one hand on Josh's hip and the other on his shoulder to hold him steady, and then he started to fuck him in earnest. There was nothing slow or tender about this tonight. It was a means to an end as he fucked out his anger and frustration, chasing his climax as if it were the only thing he wanted from Josh.

*That's all this is. That's what we're here for.*

He focused on his own needs, trying not to think about Josh as anything other than a willing body. He could tell Josh was getting off on it, though. Rupert knew the sounds Josh made, knew when he hit his prostate just right, and it was obvious Josh was getting close from the muttered curses and the flush that painted the back of his neck.

"*Fuck*," Josh gasped after a particularly brutal thrust. "You're gonna make me come."

Rupert didn't reply, but he snapped his hips harder, faster, feeling his own orgasm building. Josh dropped down onto one elbow, reaching between his legs with his other hand. He came almost immediately, squeezing Rupert's cock tight as he pulsed around him with a muffled curse. Rupert fucked him right through it, so close now he didn't want to stop. Josh moaned, and Rupert knew he was probably oversensitive, but Rupert was right there, a few more thrusts would do it. He had both hands on Josh's hips now, holding him steady as he ploughed into him. Josh tensed his muscles again, squeezing Rupert and forcing him over the edge. Rupert drove in one last time, stilling as his cock pulsed and he emptied himself into the condom with a loud groan.

The room was silent save for their harsh breathing, and they were both still for a moment.

Rupert's anger was all gone now, replaced by emptiness. He released his death grip on Josh's hips and winced at the red marks he'd left, sharp crescents where his nails had bitten into the skin. He smoothed his hand over Josh's back and up to his shoulder.

"Thanks." Rupert squeezed, feeling the bones beneath the skin and muscle.

His cock was softening now, but before he pulled out, he wanted to cover Josh's body with his own, to press apologetic kisses to his inked skin, to whisper pointless words of affection. Instead he withdrew carefully and went to the bathroom to wash his hands, unable to face Josh yet.

When he returned, Josh was lying on the bed, curled on his side, facing Rupert. He'd put his underwear back on, but the rest of his clothes still lay on the floor in a crumpled heap. Rupert had rearranged his clothing now and was still fully dressed. He hadn't even taken his shoes off. He stretched out on his back beside Josh, not touching him, just staring at the ceiling.

"Want to do anything else?" Josh asked. "You've still got some time left."

"No." Rupert hadn't meant to snap, but the word came out sharp and ugly. He sighed, forcing himself to lighten his tone before he spoke again. "Are you busy next weekend?"

"I'd need to check. Why?"

"I have a proposition for you."

"Go on," Josh said cautiously.

"I need a date for my mother's wedding. I was hoping I could book you for the weekend. There's a dinner on the Friday night and the wedding on Saturday. Two nights in a hotel — which I've paid for already. So if you can do it, I need to know how much you'd want for the whole weekend."

There was a long pause before Josh said, "It would be a lot."

"I know. But I don't care. The person I was going to take can't make it anymore, and my mother will kick up a fuss if I mess up the numbers at this late stage. Anyway, I'd rather not go to it alone. Moral support is always good when dealing with my mother and her fiancé." He tried to pass it off as a joke, but maybe something in his tone gave him away, because when Josh replied, his voice was softer than before.

"I'll do it."

"I thought you needed to check you were free?"

"I can reschedule."

"How much, then?"

Josh was silent for a moment. Rupert turned his head to see his face, and Josh was frowning, deep in thought.

"I'll do the whole weekend for two-and-a-half thousand," he finally said.

Rupert didn't care how much it would cost. He'd have paid twice that if Josh had asked. He'd be with Rupert for nearly forty-eight hours, after all.

"Okay." Rupert registered the surprise on Josh's face and realised Josh had been expecting him to balk at the price. "Cash, as usual?"

"Not for that much. I'll give you my bank details. Do you think your dad would approve of how you're spending your inheritance?" Josh's tone was light, but with a hint of something sharper that cut Rupert along with the words.

Rupert started at the ceiling again. Being with Josh made him happy — well, it had done until now — and his dad has always wanted him to be happy. "I don't think he'd care," he said gruffly. "Anyway, it's irrelevant. The money's mine to do what I like with."

*And I like you.* The words were on the tip of Rupert's tongue but went unspoken.

"So what are the arrangements for next weekend?" Josh asked.

They discussed practical stuff like travel and timings for a while. Rupert was driving, so he would give Josh a lift. They'd leave Friday lunchtime and travel back on Sunday morning. The wedding was taking place in a large country hotel near London, so it was nearly a four-hour drive.

"And how are we going to play it?" Josh said.

"What do you mean?" Rupert frowned.

"As far as the other guests are concerned, what are we to each other?" Josh sounded impatient. "I assume you don't want them to know I'm an escort. So am I there as your friend, your boyfriend, your significant other? How affectionate do you want me to be in public?"

"Oh. Um… boyfriend, I suppose." Rupert's cheeks heated. The words felt like an admission. "I think that's what people would assume anyway if we're there together."

"And you're out? Is your mother going to be okay with you bringing me? Not that it's my business, but I want to know what to expect."

"Yes. She knows I'm gay." It was a lie by omission. But Rupert didn't want to risk Josh changing his mind. He'd deal with his mother when he had to. He didn't think she'd ruin her own wedding by making a scene about Rupert bringing Josh instead of the "nice girl" she'd suggested.

"Okay. I think our hour must be up," Josh said. "I'd better get going." He got up and started pulling on his clothes.

Rupert watched him, hating this new distance between them. It was as if Josh was slipping away from him, despite his agreement to go away with Rupert next weekend. Maybe Rupert needed to accept he could never get what he wanted from Josh. But he was still clinging to a thread of hope that there was a way through this to something better. Perhaps once the wedding weekend was over, he'd find a time to broach the subject with Josh and be honest about his feelings. Unless Rupert asked Josh for more, he'd never know if it was within his grasp.

He stayed on the bed until Josh was dressed and ready to go.

"I'll see you Friday," Josh said.

"I'll be in touch about timing and lifts. If you want me to pick you up from your place, you'll need to give me the address." He wondered whether Josh would. Maybe he'd insist on meeting somewhere neutral in his bid to keep Rupert at arm's length.

But Josh nodded. "Sure. I'll text it to you."

That Josh would trust him with his address gave Rupert hope. He stood and walked over to Josh, putting his hands on his shoulders and leaning in to claim a kiss — the first kiss of the night. Josh made no move to hold him, but he kissed Rupert back. When Rupert pulled away, Josh's gaze was soft in a way that made Rupert's heart twist.

"Bye, then," Josh said.

Rupert let his hands drop. "Bye."

When the door closed behind Josh, Rupert stared at it for a long time, wondering what the hell he was doing.

## CHAPTER ELEVEN

Josh got home at half past nine. He bypassed the sounds of people in the living room and went up to his room. He was tired, but didn't think he'd sleep well tonight.

Rupert had been so cold tonight. It had felt so wrong after the intimacy of their previous encounters. But the sex had been good despite that. Josh's body responded to Rupert even when his heart wasn't in it. Josh had no idea what was going on Rupert's head. He wasn't sure he wanted to know. At least he'd been able to keep his own feelings hidden.

He was already regretting agreeing to go to the wedding with Rupert next week. What the hell was he thinking? He'd been trying to put some distance between them and get their relationship back to a purely professional basis. Spending a weekend masquerading as Rupert's boyfriend wasn't going to help with that — even if technically it was a business arrangement. Josh's feelings for Rupert were out of control, and he wasn't sure he'd be able to hide them for a whole weekend.

Josh tried to read, but he couldn't concentrate. His mind kept going back to Rupert, so he went back downstairs, hoping some company would take his mind off things.

"Hi." "Hey."

Jez and Mac greeted him in unison as he went into the living room. They barely glanced up from the screen, controllers in hands as the whine of vehicles filled the room. Jez cursed as a car in one half of the screen got blown up in the air.

"You fucker." He nudged Mac in the ribs. "Was it you who threw that blue shell at me?"

"Yep." Mac's character went zooming past Jez's and over the finish line. He tossed his controller aside and did a fist pump while Jez crossed the line in third place.

"You wanna play?" Mac asked Josh.

"Yeah, go on then." *Mario Kart* sounded like the perfect distraction. Jez moved closer to Mac to make room on the sofa for Josh.

They played for ages. Josh totally lost himself in the game. He wasn't as good at it as Jez and Mac were — they played way more often than he did — but as he got a feel for it again, he started to do better.

Mac and Jez were insanely competitive, constantly trash-talking each other and laughing if the other got blown up or knocked off the track. When they finally got tired of the game and put their controllers aside, Mac put an arm around Jez and pulled him close. Jez snuggled in with his head on Mac's shoulder and yawned.

"I'm knackered."

Mac dropped a casual kiss on the top of Jez's head. "Yeah. Bedtime soon."

Josh felt a flood of longing at the easy affection between them. There had been moments when he'd felt that with Rupert, but never for long — there was always a distance between them that couldn't be bridged.

"I'm tired too. I'm gonna head up now." Josh stood.

"Are you all right?" Jez furrowed his brow and studied Josh in a way that made Josh want to squirm. Jez was pretty perceptive.

"Yeah, I'm fine. Just tired."

"Look… mate. I know you normally talk to Dani, but she's away this weekend…. I just want you to know you can talk to us too — if you wanted."

Josh appreciated the offer, but the *us* twisted the knife a little deeper.

"Cheers. But I'm fine, honestly." He forced a smile, then added, "Night. Sleep well."

Josh showered the scent of Rupert off his skin before bed, so when he pulled the covers over him, all he could smell was his own shower gel. He lay on his back and stopped fighting the loneliness that he normally kept at bay. It swept over him like a cold grey mist, sending creeping tendrils into every corner of his psyche. His chest ached, and he curled onto his side, hugging his pillow and staring into the darkness. He wasn't sure he could go on like this.

His mind started to turn over with possibilities. Maybe he could get a different job for his final year, manage with less money. If he was working in a bar or a shop in his free time, it would be easier to meet someone, to have a real relationship. He tried to imagine what it would be like. He'd have to work longer hours, but maybe it would be worth it if he got to have someone to sleep with afterwards, to spend time with like Jez did with Mac.

The shadowy figure of Josh's imaginary future boyfriend morphed and took shape in his mind. Broad shoulders and wild red hair, a huge smile and eyes the colour of the sea.

Josh sighed. He didn't want some random guy. He wanted Rupert.

The next morning, Josh woke feeling groggy. He'd slept badly and was still tired, but once he'd woken, he couldn't get back to sleep.

Josh got his phone and checked his calendar. He'd booked in Michael for next Saturday, so he emailed to cancel, apologising and claiming a family commitment. Michael knew nothing about Josh's background, so he wouldn't know any different.

Next he checked his emails and found he had a few unanswered ones from clients. He'd been spending so much of his time with Rupert recently, he'd been neglecting the others. What with Rupert and his exams, it had been a few weeks since Josh had seen anyone else.

Philip wanted to know if Josh was free on Thursday night, because he was in town on business again. Josh also had an enquiry from a potential new client asking about his general availability. He replied to the new guy first, telling him he was very busy for the next couple of weeks but that he'd get back to him. Then he pulled up Philip's message again. He hesitated for a few moments before typing *Sorry, I can't do this week.* And then he pressed Send.

He didn't give a reason. Philip wouldn't expect one. He had never pried into Josh's private life, just as Josh never asked about his.

He flopped back on his bed and rubbed his eyes. He should have said yes to Philip and the new guy. Now term was over, Josh had plenty of time on his hands and he could see clients every day if he wanted to. But he couldn't face the thought of it. He didn't want to have sex with anyone apart from Rupert.

"I'm so fucked," he muttered in frustration.

Once this stupid wedding weekend was over, he was going to have to sort his head out. If he couldn't deal with his feelings for Rupert then he was going to have to stop seeing him. He couldn't afford to be feeling this way, not when he had another year of uni to get through before he could look for a full-time job. Even then he had to hope he could find something good enough to live on, otherwise he'd be stuck fucking and sucking for money till he was old and grey. He chuckled mirthlessly at the thought.

Dani came and sat on Josh's bed while he packed on Thursday night.

"Are you sure this is a good idea?" she asked for what felt like the hundredth time.

"No," he replied honestly. "It's probably a stupid idea, but he's already paid me." Josh had checked his bank account earlier and found the money already in his account. "Anyway, I'm not going to cancel on him now. That would be a shitty thing to do."

Rupert obviously didn't have an easy relationship with his mother and soon-to-be stepfather. If Rupert wanted Josh for moral support, then Josh wasn't going to let him down.

"But once this weekend is over, I'm going to try and stop seeing him, or maybe cut him down to once a fortnight or something."

"Can you afford to?"

"Yeah. I have plenty of other clients to fill the gap."

Dani snorted. "That's what she said."

"Oh fuck off." Josh threw a pair of balled-up socks at her, but he laughed too. "Now... which tie should I wear with the suit?"

Josh had got Dani to go shopping with him to help choose a suit for the wedding as he didn't have anything appropriate to wear. He'd gone for a classic slate grey that would do for job interviews next year. He'd also chosen a couple of different ties and was still undecided which looked best.

"The green one. It looks great with your eyes," Dani said.

"Okay." The green tie went in the case. "And what should I pack for Friday night? Rupert said smart casual for dinner. But that will be the first time I meet his mother, so I want to make a good impression. I was thinking black trousers and a shirt, but no tie. I button it high enough, it will cover my tattoos."

"Sounds good. Which shirt?"

Josh got out a couple of choices from his wardrobe: a plain greyish blue and a white one with a bird print in grey, black, and blue. He held them up for Dani's opinion.

"The one with the birds on," she said decisively. "Plain colour with the black trousers looks too much like a uniform, and I really like that one."

"You don't think it's too... I don't know. Too bold?"

"Josh, you need bold. You look unconventional, no matter how much you dress up. That shirt suits your style. Are you keeping your piercings in?"

"Yeah. Rupert didn't say anything about it, so I'm assuming it's fine. If he wanted a date without holes in their face, then he should have hired someone different."

Rupert picked Josh up at noon on Friday. Josh was waiting in the living room with his case. Jez was in there too—he'd been pumping Josh for information all morning. Josh had finally relented and told him about the wedding, but not that he was being paid to go with Rupert. So of course Jez now assumed Rupert and Josh were serious, and he was desperate to catch a glimpse of him.

Jez went to the window and peeked through the net curtains. "Ooh, your mystery man's hot, Josh. Very nice indeed."

Josh picked up his suitcase and went to open the door.

"Hi," he greeted Rupert.

Rupert leaned in for a kiss, and something in Josh relaxed a little. He was glad they seemed to have got past the awkwardness of their last meeting. He couldn't handle a whole weekend of skirting around each other. If he was going to play the role of Rupert's boyfriend convincingly, they'd need to be okay with touching each other when they weren't fucking. Josh put his case down, so he could put his hand on Rupert's waist, and he kissed him back.

When they separated, Rupert glanced sideways at the front bay window. "Did you know your housemate is spying on us?"

"Yeah. That's Jez. He thinks you're my new boyfriend, and he's excessively invested in our relationship." Josh glared at Jez, who grinned unrepentantly and waved.

Rupert's smile faltered a little. "Are you ready to leave?"

"Yes."

"Let me take that." He took Josh's case before Josh could object and carried it over to his car.

"Nice wheels," Josh said as Rupert opened the boot of a shiny silver Golf. According to the plates, it was only a year old.

"Thanks." Rupert rearranged his own luggage before sliding Josh's case in.

Josh got in the passenger side, and Rupert slid into the driver's seat and then started the engine.

"Put some music on if you want," Rupert said.

Josh started scrolling through Rupert's iPod to find something he fancied. "Any requests?"

"I don't mind. You can choose."

Josh scrolled through by artists, but didn't make it past *A* because he found the Arctic Monkeys and settled on that.

"This is good driving music, I reckon."

"Oh yeah. Nice choice."

They sat in silence for a while. Josh pushed his seat back a little more so he could stretch his legs out, and adjusted the air con to get some cold air on his face. It was hot today and the sun was blazing. He watched the houses and streets of Plymouth pass by and listened to the beat of the music and the purr of the engine. When they joined the dual carriageway, the views changed to green fields and occasional patches of woodland as they drove through Devon towards Exeter.

"So," Josh said eventually. "Is there anything I need to know? You've told me about your mother and her fiancé—Charles, is it?" Rupert nodded. "Is there anyone else significant I should know about?"

"Not really. I don't have any brothers or sisters. The only other relatives will be my aunt and uncle, but I hardly know them. I haven't seen them since my dad's funeral. They have two teenage kids, so I suppose they'll be there. But again, I'm not close to them.

"It's mostly going to be my mother and Charles's cronies—friends from her gym, and from the committees she's involved in, along with some of his colleagues. I expect there'll be a few older friends who knew my father too, but she hadn't kept in touch with many of them. My godparents will definitely be coming, though. Bill and Justine."

"What are they like?"

"They're lovely, but I haven't seen them in a long time. Not since I left London. I used to go over to their place for dinner sometimes when I was a student. Bill was a father figure for me after I lost my dad."

Rupert was quiet for a moment, but he was drumming his fingers on the wheel and Josh could see the tension in his shoulders and a muscle working in his jaw.

"What's up?" Josh asked.

Rupert let his breath out in a huff and his gaze flicked sideways for a moment before settling back on the road. "There's something I didn't mention before that I should probably warn you about...."

"Yes?"

"My mother's expecting me to turn up with a woman." The words came out in a rush. "She knows I'm gay, but she also knows I'm single, so she suggested I brought a 'nice girl' as my plus-one. I was going to take Georgina, but she couldn't make it."

Josh snorted. "Seriously? They're expecting a nice girl, and you're bringing me? I think a gay escort is about as far removed from a nice girl as you can get."

Rupert chuckled, and Josh couldn't hold his amusement in anymore. They both laughed until tears were streaming.

"Oh God. Don't!" Rupert wiped his eyes with the back of his hand, still laughing weakly as he tried to stay focused on driving. "I know. I probably should have warned her, but I couldn't face the aggro."

"So you thought you'd just turn up with me on your arm and deal with the fallout?"

"Basically, yes. My mother's all about keeping up appearances, so she won't cause a scene in front of the other guests. I reckon we can get away with it. And honestly? I think it serves her right for putting pressure on me to take a woman as a plus-one in the first place. I'm sure she only said it to try and keep Charles happy, and frankly they can both fuck off. I'm not going back in the closet for them."

"Good for you," Josh said. "You shouldn't have to."

"Thanks." Rupert gave Josh a quick smile, then added in a soft voice as he looked ahead again, "I'm really glad you agreed to this."

Josh looked at Rupert's profile, the straight nose, and the dark red hair curling on his collar. "I reckon it might be fun."

They made good time, pulling into the large circular drive of the hotel at about quarter to four.

"Oh my God, this is amazing." Josh stared at the huge stone building. Climbing roses rambled up trellises, and a beautiful plant with purple flowers grew up the wall of the building itself. Set in a couple of acres of well-tended garden, it was a far cry from the functional but barren hotels he was used to.

"No expense spared," Rupert said.

*They must have serious money*, Josh thought. He knew Rupert was well off, obviously. It was clear from his flat and his car, not to mention his ability to pay for Josh on a regular basis. But this hotel was an example of wealth on a scale that Josh had never seen first-hand before.

The entrance hall was tiled in black and white, like squares on a giant chessboard, and their footsteps echoed off the high ceiling as they walked across it to the reception desk.

Rupert gave his name to the immaculate woman who greeted them and started taking some details. Josh stood beside him, looking around in wonder, distracted by the beauty of the interior. It reminded him of the inside of a stately home he'd visited once on a school trip when he was a kid.

"And your companion?"

"Uh… Josh."

Josh snapped his attention back and realised she needed his name. Of course, Rupert didn't know his surname. "Josh Morley. Sorry, I was miles away. This is such a beautiful hotel."

The woman smiled. "Thank you. It is lovely. I hope you'll enjoy your stay here, Mr Morley."

"Has the bride checked in yet? Mrs Blanchard?" Rupert asked.

"Not yet."

"And can you tell me the arrangements for the evening? She emailed me, but I forgot to print it off."

"Drinks are being served in the parlour from seven thirty, and dinner for the wedding party is booked for eight in the conservatory."

"Okay, thanks."

"Let me get someone to help you with your luggage and show you to your room. If you need anything else, don't hesitate to ask." She caught the eye of a young man in a dark blue suit with silver buttons. "Greg, take these gentlemen up to Room Sixteen please."

Greg nodded. "Can I take your cases, sir?" He addressed Rupert at first, but then he glanced at Josh. His gaze lingered, dropping to Josh's lip ring for a moment, and when he looked back into Josh's eyes, Josh caught a flicker of interest. Josh smiled, and Greg smiled back until Rupert cleared his throat.

Greg looked away quickly and picked up their cases. He led the way to the lift and stood with his back to them until the lift arrived.

They stood in uncomfortable silence as the lift rose to the floor above. Josh caught Rupert's eye in the mirrored wall and grinned innocently. Rupert didn't look amused. There was a telltale crease between his eyebrows that Josh recognised as annoyance. Josh nudged him gently, then reached down to take his hand. Rupert let him lace their fingers together and his frown lifted a little.

The corridor upstairs had a thick crimson carpet and pale gold wallpaper. It was sumptuous and elegant, and Josh felt utterly out of place. Greg stopped outside the door at the far end on the left and stood aside so that Rupert could unlock the door. It was a proper old-fashioned lock with a key on a numbered ring.

Inside, Greg put their cases by the foot of the huge four-poster bed. "Is there anything else you need?" he asked.

"No, that's everything, thanks." Rupert handed him a tip.

"Thank you, sir. I hope you enjoy your stay." He acknowledged Josh again then with a small smile.

There was still a glint in Greg's eye that Josh recognised. "I'm sure we will. The bed looks very comfortable…. Sturdy too," he added with a suggestive grin.

Greg's cheeks turned bright pink, and he licked his lips and glanced back at Rupert. "Yes. Well, then… if that will be all, I'd better be on my way."

He scurried out of the room. Josh managed to wait until the door had closed behind him before he started laughing. "Poor bloke. I couldn't resist."

Rupert was less amused. "I hope you're not going to spend all weekend flirting with the staff. You're supposed to be my boyfriend, remember?"

"Oh, baby. Are you jealous?" Josh turned to Rupert and moved in close, grabbing him by the belt loops and reeling him in so he could kiss his neck and whisper in his ear. "You don't need to worry. I'm all yours."

## CHAPTER TWELVE

Rupert's irritation eased as Josh grazed his lips over Rupert's stubbled jaw and found his mouth. Rupert hadn't like the frisson between Josh and Greg, and possessiveness surged through him along with arousal as they kissed, deep and open-mouthed.

When Rupert pulled away to breathe, Josh's eyes were dark. He kept his grip firm on Rupert's hips.

"So, boyfriend. We've got a few hours before dinner. Do you want to find out just how sturdy this bed is?"

The unpacking could wait. "Fuck, yes." Rupert kissed him again.

They undressed each other, leaving a trail of clothes as they stumbled and tripped their way to the bed between kisses. Rupert sat on the edge of the bed and pulled Josh between his spread thighs. He kissed the crest of Josh's hipbone and the smooth skin of his belly. Josh made an impatient sound and bucked his hips forward. Rupert slid his hands into the back of Josh's snug briefs and pushed them down, gripping his arse and squeezing, deliberately letting his fingers nudge into the crack as he nuzzled Josh's erection where it was still trapped in the stretchy fabric. He rubbed his lips up and down the shaft until Josh gripped Rupert's hair and thrust against him.

Rupert grinned up at him and hooked his thumbs into the elastic waistband, finally freeing

Josh's cock as he pushed his underwear down. His erection bobbed free, hard, flushed, and gorgeous, so Rupert sucked it into his mouth and went to town. He took Josh deep at first, slicking him up and getting him wet with spit, and then backed off a little to suck on the head. The muscles in Josh's buttocks clenched tight under Rupert's hands — he could feel the tension in them as he worked Josh over. He let his fingers slip deeper into Josh's arsecrack and rubbed over his hole as he sucked.

Josh groaned. "Fuck... Rupert."

Rupert carried on with what he was doing. His own cock was still in his underwear, trapped, and he didn't have hand free for it. But he could tell Josh wasn't going to last long, and Rupert wanted to make him come like this. The ring of muscle under his fingers was softening now but was too dry for him to get inside easily. So he let Josh's cock slide from between his lips and brought his fingers to his mouth instead. He sucked on them, tasting sweat and musk from Josh's body, then reach back around as he took Josh's dick in his mouth again.

Josh gasped, fingers tightening in Rupert's hair as Rupert pushed two fingers into him up to the first knuckle. Rupert paused for a moment, letting Josh adjust, but Josh muttered "More," working himself back on Rupert's fingers until they were buried as deep as they'd go. The flavour of precome exploded across Rupert's tongue on the next suck, and his mouth watered in response.

"Jesus." Josh let out a desperate chuckle as his legs wobbled. "I'm so close."

Rupert sucked harder, fucking his fingers into the tight clench of muscle as he took Josh right back into his throat with each pass. Josh started to move his hips, finding a rhythm as he thrust his cock into Rupert's willing mouth. He made desperate sounds, moans and muttered curses, and Rupert loved it. Loved that he could make Josh feel this good.

Josh came with one final thrust, gasping out Rupert's name as he spilled into his throat, legs trembling and internal muscles pulsing around Rupert's fingers. Rupert swallowed around him, the flex of his throat eliciting another groan from Josh. Rupert started to move again, sucking gently now, making sure he'd got every last drop of Josh's release before letting Josh's softening cock slip free. He looked up at Josh's face, flushed and sweaty and split by a dazed-but-sweet smile.

"Wow," Josh said. "I need to lie down. My legs are about to give out."

Rupert chuckled. He eased his fingers out of Josh's arse and patted his hip. "Come on, then." He guided Josh to lie on the middle of the huge bed. Then he finished removing Josh's underwear, still caught around his legs. Rupert took off his own boxers before lying beside Josh and pulling him into his arms for a lazy, sated—in Josh's case, at least—kiss.

Their knees slotted together, and Josh pushed his thigh between Rupert's. Rupert's erection rubbed against Josh's hip, but it was too bony there to feel good, so he brought a hand down to stroke himself. That distracted Josh, who broke away from the kiss.

"Are you…? Oh. Mmm." He hummed in what Rupert assumed was approval.

So Rupert rolled onto his back and stroked himself more blatantly. Josh's gaze fixed on Rupert's cock, and he licked his lips.

"You like watching?" Rupert asked.

"Yeah." Josh sounded a little breathless again already. When Rupert glanced down at Josh's dick, he saw it had never fully softened and was plumping up again now.

"Want me to carry on?" Rupert slid his hand slowly down his length, rolling his foreskin back to show the dark pink head. He paused and gripped tight, showing off his cock to Josh, who was entranced.

"Uh-huh." Josh reached down to grip himself and stroke slowly, not as though he had any real intent to try and come again, but like he couldn't help but touch.

Rupert drew his hand up and then down again, his breath hitching as his foreskin slid over the sensitive glans. Precome welled at the tip, and he used a finger from his other hand to smear it around. Then he took that finger down, reaching behind his balls to find his hole and press the tip of his finger inside.

"Fuck," Josh whispered. He sat up and shuffled down the bed, moving between Rupert's spread legs so he could see better. "That is *so* hot."

"Yeah?" Rupert watched Josh's rapt face as he added another finger and pushed in a little deeper, gasping at the stretch and burn, the edge of pain only turning him on more. He was close, but the expression on Josh's face made him want to string it out, to make it last. Putting on a show for Josh like this was intense, and he was desperate to please him.

Josh was stroking himself again in earnest, his cock was fully hard, and Rupert wanted it inside him so badly.

"Could you fuck me?" Rupert asked. "Even though you just came?"

Josh gave him a delightfully dirty grin. "You want this?" He held his cock at the root, pointing it at Rupert.

"Yes." Rupert's voice came out a little hoarse. God, he wanted it so badly.

"Okay. I might not come again, though... but I can definitely fuck you. Let me find lube and condoms."

Rupert stroked himself lightly as Josh quickly got supplies and then came back to kneel between Rupert's legs. He put the condom on and slicked himself up, then passed the bottle to Rupert. "Here you go. Get yourself ready for me."

"I'm ready now." Rupert pulled his fingers out. "Just fuck me." He wanted the burn and stretch. He wanted to be able to feel Josh all evening, a reminder of this while he was sitting and making polite conversation with his mother and Charles.

Josh hesitated. "You sure?"

"Yes." Rupert reached for him, pulling him down for a kiss and bringing his knees up around Josh's hips. "Now, Josh. Please."

Rupert's breath caught as Josh pushed inside, slow but steady until he was balls-deep. Josh paused, biting his lip as he waited for Rupert to adjust to the pressure and ache of being filled so suddenly. For a moment, it was almost too much. But then Rupert remembered to breathe out, and gradually the pain gave way to a deep, swelling wave of pleasure as Josh rocked carefully into him with a small roll of his hips.

"Okay?" Josh asked.

"More than okay." Rupert put his hands on Josh's arse and encouraged him to keep moving with his slow, teasing thrusts that felt amazing but weren't quite enough. "Faster," he begged.

Josh complied, kissing Rupert again, but he couldn't quite manage the pace Rupert wanted in that position. "Hang on." He pulled out and Rupert groaned in protest. Josh pulled on Rupert's legs, guiding him until he lay on the edge of the high bed, his legs on Josh's shoulders while Josh stood on the floor. "Like this."

Josh thrust into him again, not gentle or careful this time, and Rupert cried out as the sensation lit him up.

"Oh fuck!"

"Good?"

"Yeah, don't stop." Rupert put his hand back on his cock. He was leaking so much precome his hand slid easily over the skin, making slick sounds that were audible over their harsh breathing and the creak of the bed.

Josh snapped his hips hard and fast. Rupert had never been fucked like this before, with such raw power and energy. The need and tension built and took over his senses until his whole world narrowed to the dual sensations of his hand on his dick and Josh's cock in his arse. He tried to find the words to tell Josh he was going to come, but all he could do was groan helplessly as his whole body locked tight, cock throbbing in his fist as he shot all over his stomach.

"Oh yeah. Fuck, that's hot," Josh gasped, fucking him through it until Rupert went limp, limbs suddenly like lead in the aftermath.

Josh slowed his movements, gradually bringing Rupert down but staying inside him until Rupert said. "You didn't come, did you?"

Josh shook his head, panting, cheeks red with exertion. "Not yet."

"Think you can? What do you need?"

"It won't take much now." Josh withdrew, guiding Rupert's legs down carefully. "Shuffle back a bit. There." He straddled Rupert's thighs and pulled the condom off, and then started to stroke himself.

Still high from orgasm and greedy for Josh, Rupert reached to bat Josh's hand away. "Let me." He cupped Josh's balls and tugged gently. "Fuck my mouth."

Josh grinned. "Okay." They shuffled up the bed, and Rupert adjusted a pillow under his head to help with the angle. Josh gripped the headboard with one hand and guided his cock into Rupert's waiting mouth with the other. He pushed in slowly, but Rupert still choked, his gag reflex triggered as he tried to adjust. Josh tried to draw back, but Rupert gripped his hips with both hands and pulled him in. He forced his throat to open and breathed through his nose, ignoring the way his eyes watered because he wanted this. He wanted to please Josh, to have Josh use him to get off.

Josh got the message and started to do just that. He was still cautious at first, but his thrusts were slow and sure as he fucked in and out of Rupert's throat. Rupert just held on and let it happen. His fingers tightened on Josh's hips, but urging him on, not trying to slow him down. He groaned his encouragement, the sound muffled by the fullness in his throat. Saliva pooled but he managed to swallow, making Josh groan as the movement squeezed the head of his cock.

"Gonna come," Josh gasped. "Fuck, Rupert, look at you. *Fuck*."

With one last hard thrust, he stilled and his cock jerked and pulsed, spilling into the back of Rupert's throat as Rupert swallowed it down.

Afterwards, Josh tried to pull out straight away, but Rupert stopped him, keeping him there as he sucked gently on the head and dipped his tongue into the slit to catch every last drop of come. Josh was softening now, and he shuddered and gasped, oversensitive as Rupert finally let his cock slip free.

Josh collapsed on the bed beside Rupert, his head on Rupert's chest as he curled into his embrace.

Rupert's come was cooling on his belly, but he couldn't be bothered to do anything about it. Rupert slid his fingers into Josh's hair, felt sweat, and chuckled. "We're a mess."

"Mm-hmm."

Josh's arm was heavy across Rupert's chest; his breathing was already slow and deep. Getting clean could wait. Lulled by the heat of the summer afternoon and the distant sounds of the birds outside, Rupert let his eyes drift closed, and sleep claimed him.

The next thing Rupert knew was the sound of his phone ringing from somewhere on the floor where he'd discarded his trousers earlier.

"Huh?" he mumbled, his brain thick with the treacle of sleep and the soporific warmth of the room. He peeled Josh's arm off his chest and rolled out of the bed to scrabble around and find the source of the noise, but it stopped before he reached it. "God, what time is it?"

His voice was a little hoarse and his throat ached. A flood of heat rushed through him as he remembered why.

He looked at the screen: *7:40*. And that the missed call was from his mother.

"Oh shit! We're going to be late for dinner. Josh, wake up. We need to get showered and dressed right-the-fuck *now*."

Josh groaned loudly, stretching before sitting up. "How long did we sleep?"

"Too bloody long. Get in the shower. I'll text my mother, and then I'll join you."

Josh went, and Rupert typed in a quick reassurance that they were on their way and pressed Send. Thank God she'd checked up on him. They would miss drinks but should just make dinner in time. What a way to start the weekend.

Fortunately the shower was easily big enough for two and they were in and out within a few minutes.

"I was going to shave," Josh said, squinting at the faint shadow of stubble on his jaw.

"No time for that." Rupert towelled himself off vigorously and ran a comb through his wet hair.

By some miracle they were dressed and ready by five to eight. Their hair was still damp, but other than that they looked respectable. Josh was standing in front of the mirror, fiddling with the collar on his shirt. He'd buttoned it right up and was easing it away from his neck and frowning.

"Why don't you undo it a little?" Rupert's own pale blue shirt was open to show a triangle of his chest. "It's smart casual for tonight."

"But then my tattoos show."

"Josh. When I show up with you downstairs, the tattoos will be the least of our worries. She's expecting a nice girl, remember? And anyway, I'm proud to have you here as my partner. You look gorgeous, and sexy as hell with your tattoo showing. Here…." He went up to Josh and undid the top two buttons himself, and then the third, adjusting the collar until he could see Josh's pale throat and a good expanse of chest with the dark indigo wings of the swallows peeking out. He dipped his head and pressed a kiss to the warm skin. "There."

When he drew back and stared into Josh's eyes, Josh's pupils were wide and a small smile curved his lips.

"You look good too," Josh said.

Rupert smiled back. "Thanks." He took a deep breath. "Right. Are you ready to face them?"

"Not really. But I'm hungry, so let's get this over with. Will it be obvious which knife and fork to use for things? I'm not used to eating in fancy places like this."

"Start from the outside and work in, and if in doubt, copy me. You'll be fine."

"Okay. Let's go."

Rupert was nervous about facing his mother, but from the tension rolling off Josh in the lift, Josh was just as anxious. When the lift slid to a halt on the ground floor, Rupert took Josh's hand and squeezed it tightly, lacing their fingers together and leading him out into the lobby.

## CHAPTER THIRTEEN

The parlour, which turned out to be a large room at the back of the hotel, was alarmingly full of people. Josh's stomach lurched and his appetite fled. He tightened his grip on Rupert's hand as they made their way through the double doors.

"Rupert!" A commanding female greeted them as they crossed the threshold. "Thank goodness you're here, darling. I was afraid you were stuck in traffic or…." The woman's voice stopped as she took in the sight of Josh, then her gaze dropped to their joined hands, and for a fleeting moment, she looked as though she'd smelled something bad. She recovered quickly, pasting a fake smile onto her face.

Rupert cut into the awkward silence smoothly. "Mother, I'm so sorry we're a little late. But better late than never, eh? Let me introduce you to Josh Morley." Rupert released Josh so that he could shake hands, but Rupert put his hand in the small of Josh's back instead. "Josh, my mother, Mrs Blanchard… for a few more hours at least." He chuckled.

God, Rupert was good at this, Josh thought. If he didn't already know that Rupert was nervous about this evening, Josh would never have been able to tell from his behaviour.

Rupert's mother took Josh's hand in a firm grip, and her blue eyes were flinty as she assessed him and obviously found him wanting. Her gaze lingered on his lip ring before settling back on his eyes. Josh felt terribly self-conscious about his wet hair, which he was sure hadn't gone unnoticed, but he managed to smile and murmur, "It's good to meet you, Mrs Blanchard."

"Call me Geraldine," she said, her clipped accent setting Josh on edge. Rupert was a bit posh when he spoke, but he wasn't even close to this. She sounded like the bloody Queen, and looked at Josh as though he was something unpleasant she'd just stepped in. "Charles, darling?" she called over her shoulder. "Come and meet Rupert's... friend, Josh."

The man who approached was tall and imposing. He reminded Josh of a vulture, with his gaunt face and stooping frame. The dark suit he was wearing only added to the impression. Charles raked his gaze over Josh while Josh tried not to squirm or fidget. He reminded himself that this was a job. It didn't matter what these people thought of him. He was never going to be a part of their family.

"Charles Engledow." He took Josh's proffered hand in a cool, bony grip. "Pleased to meet you, Josh." He looked anything *but* pleased.

"How do you do," Josh found himself saying. The formal greeting felt unnatural on his lips, but it seemed appropriate. He spoke the line as if he were acting in some awkward sitcom. He suppressed the wild urge to laugh hysterically.

A waiter approached with a tray of something sparkling and alcoholic-looking in fluted glasses. He offered the tray to Rupert first, who took one, then to Josh, who hesitated before taking one too. He didn't want to drink it but was afraid of being rude by refusing.

Rupert raised his glass. "Cheers. Sorry we were running a little late, but it's good to be here at last."

*Liar*, Josh thought. But he raised his glass as well and took the tiniest possible sip. It was sparkling wine — champagne or similar — and very dry. He tried not to wrinkle his nose as the sharp flavour hit his tongue.

Another waiter approached. He was older than the younger man with the tray, in his forties maybe, and he radiated self-importance from every pore.

He spoke in a hushed tone to Charles, who nodded. "We'll be right through." Charles turned to Geraldine. "Shall we go through for dinner? They're ready for us."

"Absolutely," she replied sweetly, then turned to Rupert. There was a hint of ice as she added, "You made it just in time, then. No harm done."

There were about thirty guests for dinner: friends and family who lived too far away to travel here for the day tomorrow. Most of them were adults, but there were also a couple of kids — Rupert's cousins, Josh guessed. A girl of about eleven or twelve and a tall gangly teenage boy who looked as though he was wishing the ground would swallow him up. Josh sympathised.

Josh was relieved to be seated next to Rupert. The prospect of having to make polite conversation with strangers was daunting enough, even with Rupert's support. The guests were arranged around one long table with Charles at the head and Geraldine on his right. Rupert was next to his mother with Josh beside him. Josh was grateful to have Rupert as a shield between him and Geraldine. He'd found her intimidating, to say the least. The gangly boy was on Josh's other side with his sister sitting opposite. All in all, Josh felt like he'd lucked out with the table arrangement. He'd much rather try and strike up a conversation with the kids than with any of the adults—apart from Rupert, of course.

Rupert introduced him to other people sitting at their end of the table: Geraldine's sister, Anne, her husband, Richard, and their kids—Emma and Daniel. By that time Josh was struggling to remember all the names, but he hoped he'd get away without needing to use them.

A terrifying amount of shiny, expensive-looking cutlery was on the table, along with pristine, white napkins folded into stiff peaks. Josh noticed other people taking theirs and unfolding them to lay them across their laps, so he did the same. The menu, printed onto cards, marked their places. Josh studied his to give him something to focus on so he could avoid conversation for a little longer.

Waiters swept in and started pouring wine into glasses. Josh's glass of sparkling wine was still virtually untouched, so he declined when the waiter offered him more. Rupert had drunk most of his already—clearly in need of Dutch courage—and he accepted some red wine.

"What do you fancy?" Rupert asked Josh, nodding at the menu.

"I think maybe the chicken, with the mozzarella salad starter." It all sounded amazing, but Josh was too nervous to be hungry, even though it was hours since lunch.

"I think I'll have the beef," Rupert said. "And the stilton-stuffed mushrooms."

Other people around the table were having similar conversations, and soon the waiters came back and started taking orders.

With that part over, Josh dared to glance around and caught Emma's interested gaze from across the table. He smiled at her, and she flushed at being caught staring but gave him a shy grin back.

"I like your lip ring," she said. "I got my ears pierced last weekend, and when I'm older I want to get my nose done."

"Not while you live under my roof," her father said. It didn't sound as though he was joking.

Emma rolled her eyes. "When I leave home, then. Whatever. You're so old-fashioned, Dad."

"I don't know why you want to poke holes in your face anyway," he said. "It looks ridiculous."

Josh felt his cheeks heat, suddenly very conscious of the ring in his lip and the multiple holes in his ears.

"Richard." His wife's voice had a hint of steel. "Could you pass me some water please?"

With Richard distracted, Josh changed the subject quickly. He turned to Daniel beside him. "So, Daniel, is it? How many more weeks of school do you have to suffer through before you finish for the summer?"

"Oh… um…." Daniel seemed surprised to be addressed directly. Josh felt bad for invading his please-don't-notice-me shield with no warning, but he needed allies here. "I think it's about six weeks till we break up."

"What year are you in?" Josh felt like the Spanish Inquisition. Poor Daniel's ears had gone pink at the attention. But at least the conversation had moved on from body piercing and Josh had the spotlight off himself.

"Year eleven."

"So it's exam time for you, then? Bad time to be away for a weekend."

"Yeah." Daniel made a face. "I've got history on Monday. I was revising in the car on the way here today, and will be doing it all the way home as well."

Josh asked Daniel about his favourite subjects and what he wanted to study next year when he went into the sixth form, and Daniel relaxed and opened up as Josh started to feel calmer too. Maybe this evening was going to be okay, after all.

Everything went smoothly until much later when they were eating dessert. By then the volume around the table had increased significantly — probably due to the amount of wine consumed. Josh had managed to leave his glass of sparkling wine untouched, and nobody had commented on it. He'd stuck to water. Rupert had only had one glass of red with dinner. Josh noticed he'd made it last and wondered if it was in solidarity. If so, it was sweet of him.

He supposed he and Rupert should have expected awkward questions at some point. But up till now, everyone had been treating their supposed relationship like the elephant in the room. Anne was the one who finally went there.

"So, Rupert." She leaned towards him conspiratorially from where she sat diagonally opposite, but her voice was loud, clearly audible to everyone at their end of the table. "How did you meet Josh? Have you been together long?" She was smiling and seemed to have asked the question in good faith, but Josh noticed Charles frown and catch Geraldine's eye.

Rupert hesitated. "Oh, I, um... it's hard to remember, really."

Josh resisted the urge to roll his eyes. Surely Rupert would have thought up a story? But apparently not. "We met at the university," he cut in smoothly. "Through mutual friends." It was believable and probably better than telling them he had picked Rupert up in a bar, never mind the other pertinent details about their relationship — or lack of one.

"Do you work there too?" Anne asked.

"No, I'm a student — a mature student," Josh added hastily, not wanting them to disapprove of Rupert for cradle snatching as well as being gay.

Rupert surprised him by taking his hand where it lay on the table. Josh glanced at him and gave him a quick smile. Rupert's answering smile was warm before he turned his attention back to Anne. "We've been dating a couple of months."

Josh supposed that wasn't too much of a stretch of the truth.

"That's nice."

Anne sounded genuine, but Josh caught Charles's expression and was pretty sure Charles didn't share her opinion. Geraldine was acting as if she wasn't listening to the conversation, but there was no way she could have missed it.

A pause followed, and maybe Anne picked up on the tension because she changed the subject then, turning to Geraldine and asking about their plans for the honeymoon.

Rupert released Josh's hand and went back to eating his dessert, but he nudged Josh's foot under the table with his own, and pressed against it, keeping it there as he ate.

The rest of the meal passed uneventfully, and Josh was relieved when they could finally escape back to their room.

They had the lift to themselves. Rupert leaned against the mirrored wall and breathed out a huge sigh. "God, I'm glad that's over. Thank you so much."

"What for?"

"For being a perfect pretend boyfriend."

Josh grinned. "It's easy to fake it with you."

He held Rupert's blue gaze, and something passed between them. Rupert's lips quirked and parted as if he was about to say something, but then the lift shuddered to a halt and the doors slid open, breaking the mood.

In their room, Rupert undressed immediately, stripping down to his underwear and hanging up his clothes. Josh did the same. It was a warm evening and there was no air con. They'd left the window open earlier, but even with a slight breeze coming in and making the net curtain flutter, their room was hot and stuffy.

"Is it okay if I use the bathroom first?" Rupert asked, oddly formal.

"Sure."

Josh lay on the top of the bedcovers and checked his phone while he waited for Rupert. He heard the flush of the toilet and the sound of Rupert brushing his teeth. It all felt very couply and domestic. He replied to a text from Dani, who had asked how things were going. Josh typed a quick *Fine so far*.

Rupert emerged, smelling of toothpaste, and Josh took his turn in the bathroom. Rupert was in bed when he returned, but had pushed all the covers down to the foot of the bed apart from the sheet.

"Is this okay? I thought it was too hot for the rest."

"Yes, fine." Josh got in bedside him, surprised by how natural it felt when they'd only shared a bed twice before — and one of those times had been by accident, not design.

Josh lay on his side facing away from Rupert, but Rupert moved in close behind him. Not completely in contact because of the warmth of the room, he put his hand on Josh's hip and pressed a light kiss to his shoulder.

Josh wriggled back until he could feel the soft bulge of Rupert's cloth-covered dick against his arse.

"Do you want to fuck or anything?" Josh asked. He was sleepy, but he could definitely manage something if Rupert was up for it.

"No. This is perfect." Rupert sounded tired too. "Unless you want to?"

"Nah. Sleep's good for now."

Rupert rolled away to turn off the lights, then came back to his original position. The weight of his hand on Josh's hip was like an anchor, and Josh drifted off with Rupert's warm breath tickling his neck.

Josh woke to the sensations of a hard cock pressing up against his arse and Rupert's hand sliding down his belly and into his underwear, where he curled it around Josh's erection.

"Mmmph," Josh managed, moving his hips to show his appreciation.

Rupert chuckled. "Good morning." He stroked Josh's cock a couple of times, then guided him to lie on his back while he moved down the bed to tug Josh's underwear off. Rupert eased his way between Josh's legs to kiss his balls and run a teasing tongue up his to the tip of his dick. "I seem to recall I owe you a morning blow job."

"If you insist."

Josh slid his hands into Rupert's hair and held on for the ride as Rupert repaid his debt. After Josh had come, Rupert crawled up and traded lazy, jizz-flavoured kisses while he rubbed off against Josh's hip and eventually came in his underwear.

"Aren't you a bit old to be coming in your pants?" Josh teased when he felt the warm wet patch bloom against his skin.

"Don't care," Rupert muttered before kissing him again. "Feels good."

Afterwards they lay on their backs, and Josh's eyes drifted closed again. He was utterly relaxed and filled with warm contentment. Rupert took Josh's hand and stroked circles into the palm with his fingertips.

"What's the plan for today?" Josh asked.

"There's nowhere we need to be till the service at four this afternoon. Unless you particularly want to put in an appearance downstairs, I thought we could get room service breakfast, then maybe go out somewhere for lunch so we get a break from having to be sociable?"

"Sounds good to me."

They had a lovely, lazy morning in bed, eating, watching TV and chatting. The breakfast was so huge — and late by the time they ordered it — that they decided to give lunch a miss. When they finally managed to drag themselves out of bed and shower, they went for a stroll around the stunning hotel grounds.

Near the house there was a rose garden. Gravel paths led through beds containing roses in every colour Josh could imagine, and climbing roses trained over frames to form an archway over the path. The sweet scent of roses was thick in the air.

Below the rose garden, the path opened out onto a manicured lawn. An expanse of perfectly tended grass swept gently down to a rockery at the bottom, and beyond that, a steeper slope covered with rhododendrons and mature trees. They followed the path down through to where it levelled out, and found a small lake among the trees.

"Oh, look. Swans." Rupert pointed to the majestic white birds that swept towards them like stately galleons from the opposite side of the water.

"They look hungry," Josh said. "If we'd known, we could have brought our leftover toast from breakfast."

The swans watched them with their beady gazes until they gave up on Rupert and Josh as a food source, and slowly started to drift away again.

## CHAPTER FOURTEEN

When it was time to go back and get ready for the wedding, Rupert could tell that Josh was nervous about facing the other guests again.

He felt a sudden pang of guilt for asking Josh to do this. Although Josh was doing his best, it was obvious he was out of his depth around Rupert's family. Hell, Rupert found it stressful, and he'd been brought up in this lifestyle and taught which knife and fork to use as soon as he was old enough to hold them. His mother had him handing snacks around at cocktail parties when he was ten and mixing martinis at fifteen. He might not enjoy the pomp and ceremony that went along with the trappings of his family's wealth, but at least he was used to it. He could only imagine how alien it must feel to Josh, though.

They dressed in their room. Rupert was distracted, trying to sort out his tie and then fiddling with his cufflinks, so he barely noticed what Josh was wearing until he spoke.

"How do I look?"

There was an uncertainty to Josh's tone, so Rupert knew he wasn't just fishing for compliments.

The mid-grey suit set off Josh's pale skin and dark hair to perfection, and the green of the tie brought out his eyes. He was clean-shaven and he had parted and slicked back his hair instead of letting it flop over his brow like it usually did. His lip ring and ear piercings were the only things that made him look anything other than utterly conventional, and the contrast was insanely sexy. The tension in Josh's face gave away his need for reassurance, and a sudden rush of protectiveness and affection assaulted Rupert.

"You look fantastic," he said honestly.

"Are you sure?"

"Definitely. You look gorgeous, and that suit is a great fit on you. Even my mother will be impressed."

"You reckon?" Josh's cheeks flushed pink.

"Yes."

"You look good too." There was a flash of heat in Josh's eyes as he took in the sight of Rupert all dressed up. "Reminds me of how you looked the first night we met. I thought you were hot the moment I set eyes on you in the bar."

Their gazes locked for a heady moment, and Rupert flashed back to that night — the nerves and excitement, and the illicit thrill that went along with paying for sex. He looked at Josh now, and he still wanted him just as much, but his feelings had morphed into something new. Something so much more than desire alone.

Rupert moved forward and cupped Josh's face in his hands. His skin was smooth, and as Rupert kissed Josh, he smelled the tang of cologne: something citrusy and fresh that suited Josh perfectly.

Josh wound his arms around Rupert and kissed him back. It was sweet at first, but when a heat grew between them that they didn't have time to satisfy, Rupert pulled away reluctantly. "Are you ready to go downstairs?"

Josh nodded.

Rupert pressed a last chaste kiss to his lips and then took Josh's hand. "Let's go, then."

He kept hold of Josh's hand as they made their way downstairs. The ceremony was taking place in the conservatory. The room had been completely rearranged since the night before, with rows of chairs laid out to form an aisle. An usher greeted them, and when Rupert explained he was the son of the bride, the usher led them to a row at the front. Rupert stood aside to let Josh go in first so that he could get the seat by the wall, and then Rupert moved in beside him.

The room gradually filled with guests. Anne, Richard, and their children joined them in the front row, greeting them with smiles and hellos.

Josh glanced over his shoulder. "Wow, there's so many people," he whispered. "Do you know most of them?"

Rupert turned to look. There were a few familiar faces from his childhood. He caught sight of his godparents, Bill and Justine, and waved to them. But many of the people were strangers — friends of his mother's from her new life with Charles. He felt a pang of loss for his father, unexpected in its intensity.

"Not many," he admitted.

Something must have given him away in his voice or his expression, because Josh frowned and asked, "You okay?"

"It's strange for me, I guess," Rupert kept his voice low, leaning in close. "To see how much she's moved on since Dad died. I forget sometimes because I don't live at home anymore. Don't get me wrong," he added. "I'm glad she's happy. It's just...."

Josh took his hand and squeezed it tightly. He didn't seem to need Rupert to finish the sentence.

At that point, the music started and the service began.

Josh held Rupert's hand throughout, and Rupert was grateful. He could almost feel his father there watching with him. His parents' marriage hadn't been perfect, but it had lasted. His mother had been different then, softer somehow, easier to relate to. Now she was a brittle shell of a person, all glossy perfection on the outside but empty on the inside. She only seemed interested in the trappings of her wealth and the social status she'd acquired. When his dad had died, Rupert had lost his mother too.

As the afternoon passed, tension crept up from Rupert's shoulders and neck to form a band around his head. His head ached. The drinks after the ceremony weren't helping. He was dehydrated after a couple of glasses of champagne, and too hot in his suit. The strain of maintaining his social smile and making polite conversation was getting too much, and he had the desperate urge to escape. If it wasn't for Josh, a constant presence by his side, he didn't think he'd be able to get through it.

As he introduced himself to his mother's friends from bridge and croquet, and to Charles's business associates, Rupert never shied away from introducing Josh as his boyfriend. The reactions varied from thinly veiled embarrassment to overeffusive enthusiasm and unsolicited anecdotes about their various gay friends, relations, or colleagues.

The only people who were genuinely pleased to meet Josh were Rupert's godparents, Bill and Justine. Bill shook Josh's hand and Justine gave him a hug, and they chatted for a while. Rupert relaxed a little as the conversation flowed easily, and even managed to smile back when Josh gave him a small grin of encouragement.

When Josh excused himself to go to the toilet, Justine turned to Rupert and said, "You look so happy together. It's good to see. He's lovely, Rupert."

Conflicting emotions rushed through Rupert. Pleasure that someone whose opinion he cared about liked Josh, shame at the deception, and hollow longing for the false reality he'd created.

"He is." He swallowed hard against the lump her words had caused in his throat. "He's great."

"He's a very bright young man." Bill sounded approving too. "Your father would have liked him."

Rupert couldn't manage a reply to that, so he gave an awkward nod and half smile before taking another gulp of his drink. Someone had refilled his glass again while he was chatting, but as the alcohol coursed through his system, he was glad of it.

Thankfully they were seated at a table with Bill and Justine for dinner, along with Daniel and Emma, whose parents were on the top table with the bride and groom. Rupert couldn't have picked a better group of people to be sitting with if he'd tried, and he offered grateful thanks to the universe for not putting him and Josh with some of the awful people they'd met earlier.

Everything went smoothly, and Josh seemed much more relaxed than he'd been at the meal last night. Rupert saw him hesitate uncertainly over his cutlery once or twice, but Rupert made sure he was always quick to start eating so that Josh could follow his lead. Josh stuck to drinking water as always, leaving the wine in his glass untouched, but nobody seemed to notice. If they did, they didn't mention it. Rupert drank some water, but the wine was too delicious to waste so he drank that too. Now he was starting to enjoy himself a little, the buzz from the alcohol was welcome, sending out warm tendrils of cheer and exuberance and chipping away at his natural reserve.

The after-dinner speeches were long. Rupert let his knee drop sideways until it pressed against Josh's leg under the table. He reached for Josh's hand again and stroked his thumb over Josh's knuckles as he listened to Charles drone on with some golfing anecdote about his mother. Josh's fingers were strong and slim as they played with his hand, and Rupert's mind went to dirty places. He must have completely missed the punchline of Charles's story, because everyone burst out laughing. Rupert faked a laugh too, but Josh nudged him and whispered, "You didn't hear any of that, did you?"

"Nope," Rupert admitted, getting lost in Josh's eyes for moment. "I was too busy thinking about you."

Josh flushed, but couldn't stop the shy smile that spread across his face.

Rupert wanted to kiss him so badly.

Once the meal was over, the party moved to what was rather grandly called the Ballroom. The high-ceilinged room had huge double doors that opened out onto the garden. By now Rupert and Josh had both shed their jackets and loosened their ties, and Rupert was grateful for the slight breeze drifting in from outdoors. It carried the summer scents of cut grass, jasmine, and roses — evocative and tempting. He wanted to take Josh's hand and pull him out into the twilight, away from all the people and the noise. But he thought his mother would notice if they went missing too soon. Maybe they could escape later.

"Do you need anything to drink?" he asked Josh.

"No thanks."

"Mind if I do?"

"Of course not. But you're too heavy for me to carry upstairs later, so bear that in mind." Josh grinned.

Rupert chuckled. "Don't worry. I'm not planning on drinking too much more."

He was already tipsy, but the evening was much easier to handle through the soft-focus filter of alcohol. Full from dinner, he didn't fancy beer, so he ordered a malt whisky. At the sight of his mother approaching, he added to the girl behind the bar, "Actually, can you make it a double? Thanks."

"Rupert, Josh," His mother greeted them with a slightly too-wide smile that gave her a rather predatory look.

"Hello, Mother. Congratulations again." Rupert hadn't spoken to her since the formal greeting line after the ceremony. "I hope you're enjoying the evening."

"Oh, yes." Her smile softened a fraction. "It's been lovely. I think the caterers did a terrific job."

"Can I buy you a drink?" he asked.

"No, thank you. I had enough with dinner. Don't want to trip over my feet for my first dance as Mrs Engledow."

"That *would* be unfortunate."

"Darling." Charles came over to Geraldine's side, diverting her attention away from Rupert and Josh. He didn't acknowledge their presence at all. "The band's about to start. Are you ready?"

"Yes." She smiled up at him, took his proffered arm, and they made their way to the centre of the dance floor.

The lights dimmed and a single soft spotlight picked up the couple as they stood in a ballroom hold, gazing into each other's eyes.

She really did look happy, Rupert thought. It was a shame Charles was such a git. But he supposed it wasn't any of his business who his mother married, in the same way that it wasn't any of her business who he was sleeping with, or dating… or in love with.

Just like that, Rupert knew what this was. He loved Josh. He couldn't deny it any longer, but he had no idea how to tell him—or even if he should.

The band started playing a waltz, and Charles swept Geraldine into a graceful circuit of the dance floor as the onlookers clapped and cheered. The next couple to join them were Bill and Justine, and after that a steady stream of people gradually filled up the floor until it was a sea of moving bodies.

Rupert put his glass down. "Shall we?" He offered his hand to Josh, who looked uncertain.

"I don't know how to do that type of dancing. Twerking is more my thing than ballroom."

Rupert laughed. "Fun though that sounds — and I definitely want to see it one day — I don't think my mother and her friends are ready for that. But it's easy, honestly. I'll lead, and I don't mind if you tread on my feet."

"You should have worn steel toecaps," Josh muttered, but he gave Rupert his hand and let him guide him onto the crowded dance floor.

Rupert took Josh in his arms, ignoring the fact that a few people were looking at them strangely, and started to move. Josh made a few mistakes at first, apologising and frowning down at his feet with concentration until he picked up the gentle rhythm. Then he relaxed and met Rupert's gaze, a smile on his face.

"I think I've got it."

"Told you it was easy. You're a natural." Rupert drew Josh in a little closer, enjoying the feel of Josh's lean back under his palm, the tight grip of their hands. They were moving as one now, perfectly in sync, and Josh was still smiling. His expression was so open and joyful that Rupert's heart skipped a beat.

They stayed on the floor for the next dance too, and the next. The band changed to swing after the waltz, and although they didn't know the steps, they muddled through by watching and copying what some of the others were doing.

"Am I still being the girl?" Josh asked.

Rupert chuckled. "I'm not sure. I think we've gone kind of freeform now."

The people who'd stared at them earlier had got over the novelty of a same-sex couple on the dance floor, and nobody was paying them much attention. Rupert was enjoying the liberation of being himself, dancing openly with a man at his mother's wedding. He caught Charles's eye a couple of times and saw more than a hint of disapproval in the tightness of his jaw. But Rupert was past caring. If he had a problem with them, he could fuck off.

He lost track of time. But after a while they were both hot and thirsty, so they went to the bar again. Rupert's whisky was still standing there from earlier, but he ordered water now, wanting something to refresh him before they returned to the dance floor.

"Want to go outside to cool off?" he suggested after they'd drained their glasses.

Josh nodded, so they walked out through the double doors onto the terrace. It was almost dark now, a perfect summer's night with stars beginning to pinprick the deep blue velvet of the sky. A few other people were enjoying the cooler air outside, but Rupert didn't want to make conversation. He wanted Josh all to himself for a little while. He took Josh's arm and guided him down the steps and onto the path that led through the rose garden. As soon as they were hidden from view, he stopped, reached for Josh, and pulled him into his arms. He cupped Josh's cheek with one hand, rubbed his thumb lightly over Josh's cheekbone, and stroked his eyebrow with a fingertip, tracing out Josh's features, which were almost invisible out here in the darkness. So familiar to him now, Rupert didn't need light to be able to picture Josh's face. He closed his eyes and pressed their mouths together. The kiss was soft and gentle, a slow slide of lips and tongue that sent a lazy swell of arousal through Rupert, along with a sharper longing for something more.

He pulled away, smiling at Josh's reluctance to separate as his hands gripped Rupert's waist. Rupert leaned in for another quick kiss.

"I've been wanting to do that all evening," Rupert whispered.

"Me too."

Rupert reached for Josh's hand and led him to a bench he remembered from earlier. They sat and stared out over the dark lawn.

"Look," Josh pointed to where the moon was just rising over the trees below them. Huge and almost full, it cast a silvery light that tipped the blades of grass and shone in Josh's eyes. "It's beautiful."

Rupert put his arm around Josh. Josh leaned in close, his head on Rupert's shoulder.

They sat and watched the moon rise. The scent of the roses was stronger by night, a sweet, heady scent that invaded Rupert's senses. His heart lifted along with the moon as they watched it break free of the branches and edge its way into the sky. With Josh warm by his side and his hair tickling Rupert's cheek, Rupert didn't think he'd ever experienced such a perfect moment. The only thing that could make it better would be if Josh felt the same.

When they went back inside, Rupert's euphoria persisted. A little drunk and high on the emotions racing through his system, it was easy to pretend this was real. He held Josh close as the band played something slow and gentle, closed his eyes, and imagined his feelings were reciprocated.

*I love you.* The words were bursting to come out of him, and he knew they were true.

Josh's cheek brushed his, and without thinking, Rupert drew back to find Josh's lips. He kissed him chastely, nothing more than a light brush of his mouth, but it wasn't enough. He kissed Josh a little harder, until Josh parted his lips and their tongues touched for a fleeting moment. Sighing reluctantly, Rupert drew back. If he went too far down that road, it would be almost impossible to stop.

Just then, a firm hand on his shoulder made him start, their gentle sway to the music interrupted.

"Must you?" Charles's face was flushed — with anger or alcohol, Rupert couldn't tell — and his voice was thick with disapproval. "Save it for your room, for God's sake."

"What?" Rupert blinked at him, his brain taking a while to catch up as disbelief, followed by a wave of cold fury, swept through him. He was dimly aware of his mother hovering behind Charles, her face anxious and strained. "What the hell is that supposed to mean?"

"Are you going to make me spell it out?"

They'd both kept their voices low but were already attracting attention. Other dancers close to them threw worried glances their way.

Rupert deliberately raised his voice now, tired of putting up with Charles and his snide comments and disapproving glances. "I think perhaps you should, Charles. Because I can't see a problem here."

"Rupert." Josh gripped his arm tightly, fingers digging into his bicep, a note of warning clear in his tone. "Just leave it."

"Charles, that's enough. Please," Geraldine said, tugging on Charles's elbow.

But Rupert wasn't prepared to drop this, and it seemed Charles wasn't either. Rupert glared at him, waiting for him to explain.

"You're making people uncomfortable," Charles said, his voice like ice.

"By kissing my boyfriend?" Rupert said, disbelieving. "I don't think most people were bothered. Seems to me you're the only one who wants to make an issue of it."

"For God's sake, Rupert. Bringing him at all was bad enough, dropping this on your mother with no warning. It's not enough that you need to make some sort of a statement by bringing a man to our wedding, but you have to parade your relationship in front of everyone like this? Are you trying to ruin this day for us?"

Rupert clenched his fists. "It was only a kiss, just like you kissed my mother earlier in front of everyone. How is it different? Why should you be allowed to kiss her and I'm not allowed to kiss the man I'm in love with?" Rupert was shouting now, not caring that people were listening. The words spilled from him, hot and bitter. "But don't worry. We're leaving. I'm not staying here to be insulted by a homophobe."

Rupert turned to Geraldine, who was speechless. "I'm sorry, Mother." Her face registered shock and something that might have been shame, but maybe it was just embarrassment at the scene they were causing. Rupert's voice cracked as he spoke again, emotion swamping him. "We're clearly not welcome here. Come on, Josh."

Josh was staring at him, stunned and pale. Rupert took Josh's hand in a vice-like grip and pulled him towards the nearest escape route — out through the doors to the garden and into the comforting darkness that lay beyond.

## CHAPTER FIFTEEN

Josh stumbled after Rupert, tripping over an uneven paving slab as his eyes struggled to adjust to the sudden change. They half walked, half ran across the lawn and down through the rock garden to the shelter of the trees and shrubs that edged the lake. Rupert's breathing was ragged, and when they finally came to a stop, Josh realised Rupert was crying, harsh, tearing sobs.

"That fucking bastard," Rupert spat. "I'm so sorry, Josh. If I'd known it would be like this, I'd never have asked you to come. *God.*"

Josh pulled Rupert into his arms and held him tight. Rupert clung to him, his tears hot and wet against Josh's neck. Unsure what to say, Josh made soothing sounds, stroking Rupert's back and waiting for him to calm down. Josh's heart was pounding hard, and all he could think about was what Rupert had said back there in the heat of the moment. The exact words he'd used… one word in particular. Had there been any truth in it at all? Or did he just say it to prove a point?

He brought a hand up to cup Rupert's head, combing his fingers through Rupert's curls until Rupert finally gave a sniff and drew back. The moon was high now, and there was enough light for Josh to see the wet streaks on Rupert's cheeks. His heart twisted, and he pulled Rupert's face to his, kissing the tears away, then pressing his lips to Rupert's temple, breathing him in and trying to push down the surge of emotion that was threatening to overwhelm him. He wanted to focus on offering the comfort Rupert needed.

"That wasn't how I wanted to tell you," Rupert said quietly.

Josh felt as though his heart stopped for a moment, frantically trying to wrap his mind around what Rupert was saying. Surely he couldn't mean…. "Tell me what?" He needed Rupert to be clear.

"That I'm in love with you."

Josh's heart surged, tripping against his ribs and making him almost dizzy with elation. He pulled back, holding Rupert's face in both hands so he could study his expression, still almost afraid to believe his ears. Rupert was utterly calm now; the tempest of emotion had passed, leaving still waters in its wake. He held Josh's gaze, and there was nothing there to make Josh doubt him, just raw honesty and hope.

Knocked sideways by longing, all Josh could do was kiss him. Trying to say with his actions what he wasn't ready to say with words, he kissed Rupert slow and deep, pulling him in close as though he was trying to meld their bodies into one. He wanted so much. He loved Rupert too; he knew it deep down in his blood and in his bones. But how was this ever going to work?

Right now he pushed those thoughts aside as their bodies took over and reason fled. Hands tugged at shirttails, seeking skin, as they pressed together, hard and wanting.

"Rupert," Josh groaned as Rupert unzipped Josh's trousers and shoved his hand into Josh's underwear, curling around his erection and stroking.

Josh reached for Rupert too, fumbling until he had Rupert in his hand.

"Fuck, yes," Rupert muttered.

Their lips locked again in a messy kiss as they jerked each other off, chasing their climax. It was as though all the adrenaline of before, all the tangled, overwhelming emotion had led to this, this surge of desperate need and want that tore through Josh, leaving him breathless and teetering on the brink within minutes. He threw his head back and moaned as he came, slicking Rupert's fist as he spilled between them in a series of dizzying pulses. He was dimly aware of Rupert coming too, hissing out a curse as Josh stroked him through it. The scent of their come filled the space between them, and the sound of their shaky breathing was suddenly loud in the still quiet of the night air.

The tension hadn't dissipated between them. If anything, it was worse now their physical needs had been met. The silence was deafening. Josh knew he should tell Rupert how he felt. But instead he let out a shaky laugh and said, "I hope you know a good dry cleaner. Because our suit trousers are going to be fucked."

Rupert huffed a laugh and drew back. He held his hand up, and Josh could see come glistening on his fingers. "I think I caught most of yours."

Rupert stooped to wipe his hand on the grass, and Josh did the same, before straightening up and adjusting his clothes.

"Josh." His voice was serious now. "We need to talk."

Josh's stomach flipped, but he nodded. "Okay."

They made their way back up to the main garden, stepping carefully over the uneven path in the darkness. They skirted the edge of the lawn, avoiding the terrace where people had spilled out from the wedding party. Josh breathed a sigh of relief as they reached the path that led around the side of the hotel to the front entrance. The last thing he wanted now was another showdown with Rupert's shit of a stepfather.

In their room, Rupert sat on the edge of the bed and Josh took the chair by the window. There was a long pause before Rupert finally spoke.

"So. I'm officially a ridiculous cliché. Do you get many clients falling in love with you?"

"Not that I know of. I mean, you're the first one who's ever said."

Rupert gave a hollow laugh. "I guess that makes me extra stupid."

"Rupert—"

"Don't, Josh. You don't have to say anything. I know this must be really awkward for you. I wish I'd kept my stupid mouth shut, but I lost my temper with Charles and it all came out... and then I was tired of hiding it from you." He sighed, and his lips thinned, turning down at the corners. He looked so unhappy that Josh's heart ached in sympathy.

"Rupert," he said again, more insistently this time. "It's not one-sided, okay? I... I feel the same about you. It's more than a business arrangement for me." Hope was dawning on Rupert's face, so Josh carried on quickly, not wanting to let him get carried away. "But—"

"Fuck. I knew there'd be a catch."

"*But* I don't see how this could ever work. How can we go from escort and client to a real relationship? How would you cope with me doing my job? How could we ever be equals? I dunno. I just don't think it's possible." Josh's chest ached as he said the words, even though he knew them to be true.

"We could make it work," Rupert insisted. The hope in his expression hadn't died yet.

"This is real life, Rupert. Not some cheesy Hollywood flick."

"You've only got one year left at uni. You could move in with me, rent-free. I don't need you to contribute anything towards bills, and I don't have a mortgage to pay." Rupert's voice was pleading. "I could even pay your tuition fees. You don't need to keep working."

"But then I'd feel as though I *was* still working. I'd just be working full-time for you. I couldn't be dependent on you. It wouldn't be right." Josh felt awful, watching the excitement drain from Rupert's face, to be replaced by hurt.

"But that's what couples do. They support each other."

"In a long-term relationship, maybe. But not with something so new, and especially not given how we met. I couldn't live like that, feeling as if you were buying me in a different way."

"So, what are you saying? You'll be my boyfriend, but only if you can carry on sleeping with other men for money?" The bitterness in Rupert's voice stung.

"Basically yes." Josh shrugged. "Just for another year, and then, if we're still together when

I graduate, I'll quit as soon as I get a permanent job."

Rupert shook his head. "I don't know if I could deal with that. I want you all to myself."

Josh's heart squeezed. He wanted that too. He imagined how he'd feel if Rupert slept with another guy, and the thought of it was like a blunt knife to his gut. He couldn't ask Rupert to put up with that.

He sighed heavily, exhaustion overwhelming him now the adrenaline rush from the earlier drama had passed. It seemed Rupert felt the same, because he yawned. Josh noticed the shadows under his eyes and the tired slump to his shoulders.

"Can we sleep on it?" Rupert asked. "See if either of us feel differently in the morning?"

Josh nodded. "Yeah. I'm knackered."

They stripped down to their underwear in silence and shared the bathroom, moving around each other in the small space as they took turns to pee and brush teeth. It felt so domestic and intimate, and only made Josh more aware of how much he longed for what Rupert was offering. But he knew he couldn't do it on Rupert's terms.

Head aching and thoughts whirling, he lay and stared into the darkness. Rupert had curled in behind him, his arm tight around Josh's waist as if he was afraid Josh might sneak away in the night. From the rhythm of his breathing, Josh suspected Rupert was lying awake too.

Josh went over and over what Rupert had said, considering the problem from every angle as he waited for sleep to come. Maybe there was a way they could make it work.... But he needed to be sure.

## CHAPTER SIXTEEN

The next morning they were both tired and jaded. Josh had lain awake for hours in the night, and judging by how restless Rupert had been, he hadn't slept well either. Their moods were sombre, and they were quiet as they packed up their belongings ready to travel home.

They'd got up early, deciding to skip the hotel breakfast and get on the road home as soon as they could. Rupert had no desire to see his mother or Charles before leaving, and Josh didn't blame him. After the shitty way Charles had behaved last night, Josh thought the ball was definitely in their court. He hoped Rupert would eventually get the apology he deserved.

"We left our suit jackets in the Ballroom," Josh said as he loosely folded his come-stained suit trousers to shove into his case. "Shall I go down and look for them?"

"If you don't mind?" Rupert was still wearing just a T-shirt and boxers, but Josh was fully dressed. "If you see Charles, run in the opposite direction and I'll buy us both new suits instead." His lips quirked, but it only half sounded like a joke.

Josh made it downstairs without incident, but their jackets were gone. When he asked at reception, the girl behind the counter made a call to someone to ask whether they'd been found when the room was cleaned.

"Josh." A female voice made him turn; Geraldine was standing there with their jackets over her arm. There was no sign of Charles—*thank God*—and her demeanour was nervous rather than confrontational. "I picked these up last night after you left." She handed the jackets to Josh. "I... I'm so sorry about Charles, about what he said. Is Rupert all right?"

"Depends on what you mean by all right. But it's not you who should be apologising, and it's not me who needs the apology."

She flushed but held his gaze. "I know. But I *am* sorry, and I'm sorry I wasn't more welcoming to you on Friday night as well. I just wasn't expecting.... But never mind. After what Rupert said about being in love with you, I realised I was wrong. Even before he said it, I could see it in how he looked at you. I've never seen him look at anyone like that before. You make him happy."

Josh's stomach twisted. If only she knew the reality of their situation. "Maybe," he said.

"You do. I'll talk to Charles and get him to contact Rupert and make amends." There was a thread of steel in her tone. Josh met her eyes. Sky blue and determined, they reminded him of Rupert's. "Please tell him I'm sorry, that I love him, and I'm glad he's found someone."

"Tell him yourself," Josh said, but his voice was gentle. "I think he'd rather hear it from you. Our room is number sixteen. Go up now. I'll give it twenty minutes before I come back up."

Carrying their jackets, Josh went out into the garden and retraced their steps of the night before. He walked down to the trees by the lake and looked out across the water. The swans came to greet him, looking expectant.

"Sorry," he said to them. "I came empty-handed again."

He leaned against a tree and replayed the events of last night again in his head, and the conversations that had followed. He sighed. The problems they faced still seemed equally insurmountable by daylight.

When he went back to their room, Rupert was alone.

"Are you okay?" Josh asked cautiously, laying the jackets down on the bed. He hoped he'd done the right thing by sending Geraldine up to see Rupert.

"A heads-up would have been nice."

"I left my phone up here. But she seemed genuine. I thought—"

"It's fine, Josh. You did the right thing. We…. Well, we're not completely okay yet, but it's better. She likes you," he added. "She said I should hang on to you. I told her I was trying." He gave Josh a small smile that didn't quite reach his eyes.

Josh didn't know how to answer, so he turned away and busied himself with putting the last few things in his case before zipping it up.

"Are you ready to leave?" Rupert asked when he'd finished.

"Yes." Josh wanted to go to Rupert, hug him and kiss him, drag him back to bed and get lost in the physical again. All this emotional stuff was way too hard.

But instead he lifted his case and led the way out of the door.

Once they were on the motorway, Rupert raised the topic they'd both been avoiding all morning.

"So. Are we still in a stalemate situation here? My offer still stands. I want you to move in with me—as my boyfriend—and for you to let me support you through your final year. You can pay me back if you want to. Call it a loan if that makes it better?" Rupert kept his gaze fixed on the road in front as he said clearly. "I love you, Josh, and I want you in my life to stay."

Tears pricked at Josh's eyelids. Hearing the words in the daylight made them even more real. Josh had been wondering how much of Rupert's declarations last night were fuelled by alcohol as well as emotions, but now he believed him 100 percent. He could hear it in the barely concealed pleading in Rupert's tone, and read it in the tension of his hands on the steering wheel.

"I love you too." Josh had to say it back. It was true, and he owed Rupert his honesty. His throat was tight and he struggled to get the words out. "But I don't think I can accept that offer. Maybe I'm crazy not to, I don't know. I just…." He couldn't articulate it. He felt as though he was being pulled in two. His heart was pulling him in one direction, saying yes, but his brain was saying no. "Can I think about it for a few days?"

"Of course," Rupert said quickly. "I know it's a huge decision. Moving in with me would be big enough even without the rest of it."

"Yeah." Although, strangely, the living-together part was the least of Josh's worries. That part would be easy, but he needed to find a way he could move in with Rupert and feel like his equal.

When Rupert dropped Josh back home, he got out and walked him to his front door. The intensity of his gaze made Josh's heart pound and his stomach swoop. He needed time away from Rupert to think rationally, because when Rupert looked at him like that, it made Josh want to agree to everything he suggested.

"I'll be in touch," Josh promised. "Give me some space for a day or so, okay?"

Rupert nodded. "Okay." Then, oddly formal, he asked, "Can I kiss you goodbye?"

"Of course." Josh put his case down and pulled Rupert close.

As their lips met, he tried not to think about the fact that this might be the last time they did this. But if he refused Rupert's offer, they would have to stop seeing each other, for both their sakes. His heart hurt at the idea of this being over, and he twisted his fingers into Rupert's hair, kissing him harder until they were both breathless. When Josh finally pulled away, his eyes were embarrassingly damp, and he blinked away the tears that threatened.

"I'll call you soon," he said.

Rupert nodded. "Take care."

"You too."

The house was quiet when Josh let himself in. "Anyone home?" he called, his voice echoing up the stairwell. "Hello?"

There was no response. He knew Dani was away on holiday with her boyfriend now, and

Shawn and Mike had gone home for the summer, but Jez and Mac were still there. Then he remembered Mac had got some temporary construction work this week, and he guessed Jez must be working too. After losing his job at the cafe before Christmas, Jez had managed to get some shifts in a local supermarket.

Josh carried his case up to his bedroom and flopped down on his bed. He couldn't be bothered to unpack, and exhaustion was catching up with him after his shitty night's sleep. It was warm in his top floor bedroom, and tiredness rolled over him like a wave, making him yawn as his eyelids began to droop. He curled onto his side and hugged his pillow to his chest, closed his eyes, and slept.

When Josh awoke to the slam of the front door, it was late afternoon. Sweaty and disoriented, he blinked at the bright sunlight that was now slanting in through his attic window. He stood and swayed, momentarily dizzy from the sudden move from horizontal to vertical, and paused while he waited for the blood to reach his brain. Then he stumbled over to open his window and let some fresher air into the stuffy heat of the room. A bottle of water stood on his desk; his mouth was dry, so he opened it and drank. Lukewarm, but still refreshing, he could almost feel the liquid reaching his bloodstream and then his brain, waking him up and clearing his sleep-addled thoughts.

His stomach growled, reminding him he'd skipped breakfast and slept through lunchtime.

He went downstairs and found Jez in the kitchen, frying bacon and buttering slices of bread. The smell of the bacon made another pang of hunger clench at Josh's gut.

"Hi." Jez grinned. "How are you? Did you have a good weekend with your bloke?"

"Um... yeah. I guess." Parts of the weekend had been good, he supposed.

"Lots of hotel sex?"

"Some." Josh smiled, remembering the fumble in the woods last night and wondering whether that still counted. He went to the fridge and stared at his almost-empty shelf. A lump of questionable cheese rubbed shoulders with a tired-looking half cucumber and some hummus that was probably past its best. He really needed to go shopping later. "Can I nick a couple of pieces of bread? I'm out of everything."

"Sure, help yourself."

Josh fixed himself some cheese on toast while Jez finished making his bacon sarnie. They ate their food in the living room with the telly on, as usual. Jez was watching some US comedy on Netflix, but Josh wasn't paying any attention to it. His head was too full of thoughts of Rupert.

"Josh!"

"Huh?" He belatedly realised Jez was addressing him.

"Are you all right, mate? You were miles away. You seem a bit preoccupied."

Josh sighed, and put his empty plate down so he could curl his knees up and snuggle down into his corner of the sofa.

"Yeah. No. I don't know."

Jez hit pause on the remote and turned to look at Josh questioningly. "Man trouble? Wanna tell me about it?"

Josh considered. He could use someone to talk this through with, and the obvious person—Dani—

wasn't around. "It's a long story," he hedged, wondering whether he could trust Jez not to judge him, because there was no way he could explain the problem without fessing up to his escort work. He reckoned Jez would probably be cool.

"Mac's working late, and I have time on my hands." Jez shifted around on the sofa, leaning back against the arm now. "Spill."

So Josh took a deep breath, screwed up his courage, and did just that.

"Wow," Jez finally said when Josh had finished filling him in. "Fuck. I can't believe I didn't know about this. All this time? That's how you've been paying your way through uni?" He seemed incredulous but not disapproving; he sounded more admiring than anything.

Josh nodded.

"And you earned enough to cover everything? I assumed you had student loans like everyone else."

"Nope. I was hoping to get through the three years without needing one."

"You do know you don't even have to start paying them back till you're earning loads, yeah?"

"I know, but why leave uni with masses of debt if I don't need to?"

"But now, if you're going to be with Rupert, you'd need to stop… turning tricks or whatever you call it."

"I call it fucking guys for money," Josh said dryly. "But yeah, that's what it comes down to. He wants me to move in with him rent-free. He'll pay my uni fees, my living costs, all of it."

Jez shrugged. "And this is a problem because?"

"Because how is that different to him paying me for sex? Maybe it will feel different to him, but I'll still feel like he owns me if he pays for everything."

"So, you're going to throw away the chance of a relationship with a guy you care about because of what? Your pride?"

Josh shrugged, irritation rising because Jez didn't get it. "But I don't see how it can ever be a healthy relationship when it started out this way."

"Relationships start in all sorts of weird ways, Josh. Look at me and Mac. We started out by wanking to porn together, and Mac wasn't even into blokes. You couldn't make that shit up. But look at us now, six months down the line and still going strong. And when I freaked out about it, because I didn't think Mac could ever want more than sex with me, *you* were the one who told me to give it a chance and be honest with him." Jez's voice rose as he emphasised the point. "You said as long as we were into each other, as long as we were good together, none of the rest of it mattered. I know your situation with Rupert is fucked up for a different reason, but I think that advice works here too. If you love each other, if you really want to be together, then you can find a way to make this work."

Jez stopped, holding Josh's gaze as Josh thought about what he'd said.

"I don't know…. Maybe you're right?"

"I *am* right." Jez grinned. "Seriously. If you like him as much as you say, you'd be mad to pass him up. If you can't deal with him being your sugar daddy, then get a loan, get a different job. Find a compromise. There has to be a way."

The seed of the idea was planted in Josh's mind, and it germinated, spreading out hopeful shoots. "Yeah," he said. Then with more determination, "Yeah. Okay. I'm going to look at my finances and see what I can work out." He got up from the sofa. "Thanks, Jez."

Jez held his hand out for Josh to high-five it. "You're welcome. I owed you one."

Josh chuckled. "Yeah, you did. I got your head out of your arse about Mac, so now you're returning the favour."

## CHAPTER SEVENTEEN

Rupert slumped on his sofa, feeling as flat as a burst balloon. He couldn't settle to anything, he had no appetite, and he didn't know what to do with himself. It was almost bedtime now, but he didn't think he'd be able to sleep. All he could think about was Josh and what might be going through his head right now. He wasn't sure whether Josh really meant it when he said he'd think about it, or if it was his way of letting Rupert down gently. He glared at his phone where it lay on the coffee table and willed it to ring or chime with a text message.

Just then, the buzz of the doorbell made him start. He couldn't think of anyone apart from Josh who would turn up this late at night unannounced, but he tried not to get excited as he went to the intercom.

"Hello?"

"Rupert, it's me." Josh's breathless voice made Rupert's heart surge. His hopes rose steadily as Josh added, "Can I come up? I need to talk to you."

Josh was still out of breath when Rupert opened the door to him, and his dark hair was stuck to his temples with sweat.

"Sorry. I ran all the way here."

"Let me get you a drink," Rupert said.

"No. That can wait." Josh took Rupert's hands in both of his and squeezed them so tight it hurt. "You haven't changed your mind, right? You still want us to be together… a real relationship?"

Rupert nodded.

"And are you sure it's okay for me to move in here, and it won't be too soon for us to live together?" The words spilled out as though Josh couldn't say them quickly enough. "I mean… I've paid up till the end of August for my place, but I can move in after that."

"God, yes," Rupert pulled Josh closer. "Are you sure?"

"Yeah, but we're doing it a little differently to how you planned it." Josh's face turned serious. "Your offer was amazing, and I appreciate it, really. But I need to keep some independence, so I've come up with my own plan. I'll move in here, and as you don't have a mortgage, I won't pay you rent. But I *will* contribute towards bills and living costs and stuff. I don't want to sponge off you."

"You wouldn't be—"

"It would feel that way to me," Josh said firmly. "So it's non-negotiable. And I'm gonna get a loan for my final year fees. I have some savings to cover part of it, but I'm borrowing the money to pay for the rest. Then I'll find a new job to help with bills and food. There's part-time jobs going in the supermarket where Jez works. It won't pay much, but it'll be enough." He paused for breath and then added, "So, that's it. That's my final offer. I'll move in. We can live together… be together. But you have to let me pay my way."

Josh's gaze was fixed on Rupert's. His expression was intense, almost wary, as though he was expecting Rupert to refuse him.

"Okay," Rupert said.

They stared at each other a moment longer. Josh's lips quirked, and then slowly spread into a wide, beautiful smile. Rupert felt an answering smile stretch across his face.

"Okay," Josh repeated. "Well, I'm glad that's settled."

Rupert's happiness welled up and overflowed into laughter. He pulled Josh into his arms and buried his face in Josh's neck. The warm, perfect scent of him reached down and curled around Rupert's chest, tightening in a band around his lungs. Rupert swallowed against the sudden lump in his throat, and his eyes prickled. The laughter turned into a shaky sigh.

"Hey." Josh turned his face, nuzzling against Rupert's stubbled jaw. "You're supposed to be happy." But his voice was a little choked too.

"I *am* happy, you idiot," Rupert said gruffly. "I was just so fucking scared you'd say no. So please allow me a moment here."

He slid his hands down Josh's back, tugging him closer, then slipped his hands into Josh's back pockets, feeling for his arse. But the fingertips of one hand met folded paper.

"Oh, yeah," Josh said. "That's for you."

"What is it?" Rupert pulled whatever it was out of Josh's pocket and held it between them so he could see. It was a wad of ten-pound notes, fresh from a cash machine by the look of it.

Josh grinned. "It's the two hundred quid I owe you."

Rupert frowned. "I don't understand."

"Well… the first night, when you picked me up in the bar—"

"I think you'll find it was *you* who picked *me* up," Rupert said.

"Whatever. Anyway. That's not the point. The point is I lied to you… about having a hotel room to pay for. Philip had already paid me in advance, so I didn't need your money that night."

Rupert bristled at the mention of Philip's name. "I don't care. I don't want it back." He tried to press the notes into Josh's hand. "Keep it."

"No," Josh said sharply. "It's yours. Please, Rupert. Take it. I wish I could pay you back for all the other times you paid me, but that's not possible. But for our first night, I can."

Josh's eyes were pleading, but the determined set of his jaw told Rupert it wasn't a battle he was going to win. It was important to Josh that Rupert let him pay him back.

"Okay." Rupert put the cash in his own pocket.

Josh rewarded him with a smile. "I love you."

Rupert kissed the words from his lips as a fierce surge of love and possession rippled through him. "I love you too," he muttered between kisses. "So much." He was already backing Josh towards the bedroom, tugging at his clothes, trying to get to his skin. "Now let me take you to bed and show you."

"Yes please."

## EPILOGUE

*Three months later*

"But Rupert, we don't have time for this. We should be clearing up and getting ready, the party starts in a couple of… ohhh. " Josh's protests trailed away into a moan as Rupert dropped to his knees and parted Josh's cheeks to lick over his hole. "Okay, okay, I was wrong. There's always time for this. *Fuck*."

Josh gripped the kitchen surface tightly, his sweatpants bunched around his ankles. He briefly wondered if the tiled floor was hurting Rupert's knees before he forgot about everything apart from the hot wet slide of Rupert's tongue.

"Fuck me, Rupert, please. I want your cock," he eventually gasped. The rim job was amazing, but he wanted more. He wanted deeper, harder, *everything*.

"No lube in here." Rupert's voice was muffled in the crack of Josh's arse. "Want me to suck you off instead?"

"No. I want you in me." Josh's voice was a high-pitched whine of frustration. Why was the bloody bedroom so far away? Why didn't they keep lube in the kitchen, for fuck's sake? His eyes lit on a bottle of fancy olive oil that Rupert liked to use in salad dressings. He grabbed it and passed it back, nearly hitting Rupert on the head with it. "Use this," he said.

"Are you sure it will work? I don't want to hurt you."

"There's probably still lube up there from this morning anyway. It'll be fine. Fucking do it Rupert, now, or I swear to God—"

His words cut off abruptly as Rupert's fingers smeared the oil over his hole, and then Rupert was on his feet, the blunt head of his cock rubbing and pressing, teasing with just the tip until Josh pushed back on it, forcing Rupert to fuck him like he needed.

They'd been fucking bare for the past week since they'd both got a second round of negative tests, and Josh didn't think he'd ever get tired of the feeling of Rupert sliding into him—or vice versa—intimate skin to intimate skin, with no barrier between them. It wasn't only the physical sensation that did it for Josh, it was what it represented: exclusivity, possession, trust.

Rupert pulled Josh's hips back so that he could wrap his hand around Josh's cock and stroke as he fucked him. Rupert's fingers were slippery with oil, and they felt so good, Josh could hardly stand it. He put his head on his arms, closed his eyes, and let Rupert take him, pushing him inexorably up and up towards a peak of blinding pleasure. When Josh came, gasping and shuddering through his climax, he felt Rupert come too, cock pulsing deep where they were joined.

His legs as wobbly as a newborn foal's, Josh was glad of the kitchen surface holding him up as he gradually floated back to reality. "Jesus," he mumbled. "That was amazing." Then he started to laugh.

"What?" Rupert asked as he carefully eased himself free in a trickle of oil and come.

"Better add mopping the kitchen floor to our to-do list before people start to arrive." Josh's come was streaked white on the slate tiles by his feet. "Oh, and I got some on the cupboard door too."

Rupert chuckled and leaned low over Josh, warm breath tickling his ear as he pressed a kiss to his cheek. "I've got it. You go and have the first shower."


"Happy housewarming," Jez greeted Josh with a huge hug, releasing him with a pat on the back.

Josh hugged Mac too and then took the pack of beer he was holding out. "Thanks, I'll put these in the fridge."

"Wow, this place is amazing." Jez looked around in wonder. "Bit of a step up from our dump, huh?"

"Our place wasn't so bad," Josh said.

"Yeah, but it's nothing like this." Jez made a beeline for the doors to the balcony. "And look at the view. Oh, hi, Rupert."

Josh watched as Rupert hugged Jez and greeted Mac the same way. Rupert had met them a few times now, but he still didn't know Josh's friends well. That was the point of this evening, a bit of "cross-pollination of their friendship groups" as Rupert had called it. They hadn't invited loads of people—the flat wasn't big enough for a huge party—but they'd asked their closer friends: Jez and Mac, Dani and her boyfriend, Georgina and her new bloke, plus a few other colleagues of

Rupert's and some friends from Josh's course. About twenty people in all.

They'd asked people to bring a bottle, and had bought a ton of food. It was very civilised, definitely a step up from a student party. Josh reckoned he could get used to this.

Later in the evening, Josh was out on the roof garden talking to Georgina. It was dark and the clear September skies brought the first chill of autumn with them. Josh had just noticed he was starting to feel cold, when a strong arm slid around his chest and the warmth of a familiar body pressed up behind him. Josh snuggled back gratefully. Rupert kissed Josh's cheek. "Sorry to interrupt, Georgina. You've been out here for ages. I came to see if you needed anything? Another drink?"

Georgina chuckled, raising her glass of wine and nodding at the full glass of orange juice in Josh's hand. "You're so transparent, Rupert. Just admit you couldn't stay away from Josh any longer."

"Guilty as charged." Rupert tightened his arm around Josh.

Josh couldn't stop the smile that tugged at his lips, giving in and letting it spread.

Georgina was grinning at both of them. "You two are so adorable together," she said. "And I'm getting chilly out here, so I'm going to join the others back inside. I'll see you later." As she walked away, she paused and called back over her shoulder, "No shagging on the balcony. If you're not inside in ten minutes, I'm sending out a search party."

Josh turned, sliding his arms around Rupert's waist and leaning in to brush their lips together. "We haven't christened the roof garden yet."

Since Josh had moved in a couple of weeks ago, they'd managed to have sex in every room and on nearly every possible surface.

Rupert chuckled. "Nope. But I don't think now's the time."

"Yeah. There's no rush. We'll get to that another day."

Rupert kissed Josh again, a slow, sweet press of lips. Josh closed his eyes and kissed him back. In his imagination their future stretched out ahead of them, endless days and nights together. Josh had never imagined having this sort of happiness until it happened to him. He shivered, properly cold now despite Rupert's arms around him.

He drew away reluctantly. "Maybe next summer. I reckon it's a bit nippy for al fresco sex now."

"Want to go back in and join the party?" Rupert asked.

The sounds of their friends talking and laughing spilled out through the doors. Josh's heart swelled at the sound of it. Their lives were entwining, and it felt good.

"Sure." He slipped his hand into Rupert's and smiled at the warm tangle of their fingers. "Let's go."

## About the Author

Jay lives just outside Bristol in the West of England, with her husband, two children, and two cats. Jay comes from a family of writers, but she always used to believe that the gene for fiction writing had passed her by. She spent years only ever writing emails, articles, or website content.
One day, she decided to try and write a short story—just to see if she could—and found it rather addictive. She hasn't stopped writing since.

www.jaynorthcote.com
Twitter: @jay_northcote
Facebook: search for Jay Northcote Fiction
Email: jaynorthcote@gmail.com


Also by Jay Northcote

Novels and Novellas:
*Cold Feet*
*Helping Hand*
*Nothing Serious*
*Nothing Special*
*Nothing Ventured*
*Not Just Friends*
*Passing Through*
*The Dating Game*
*The Little Things*
*The Marrying Kind*

Short Stories:
*Top Me Maybe?*
*All Man*